VIOLENT WITHDRAWAL

Without warning a series of shots rang out. The glass door of the Bayport State Bank branch shattered into what seemed like a million fragments.

"Look out!" Frank shouted, grabbing Callie's arm.

They hadn't gotten more than three feet when a little knot of bandits in suits, ties, and ski masks burst out of the bank. One of them aimed an assault rifle at the Hardys and Callie, who were caught between them and the exit doors.

"Don't make any dumb moves," he growled. "Against the wall, now!"

Joe and Frank put their hands up and backed toward the wall slowly. Another of the robbers ran over. "Mall security's coming," he blurted out. "They're armed."

"Grab the girl," the first robber ordered. "We'll use her as a shield."

Horrified, Frank watched a second man grab Callie's arm, twist it behind her back, and put a pistol to her head.

Books in THE HARDY BOYS CASEFILES™ Series

Available from ARCHWAY Paperbacks

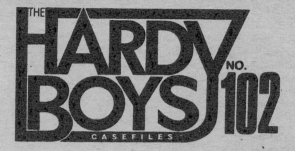

THE HARDY BOYS NO. 102 CASEFILES

WRONG SIDE OF THE LAW

FRANKLIN W. DIXON

AN ARCHWAY PAPERBACK
Published by POCKET BOOKS
New York London Toronto Sydney Tokyo Singapore

AN ARCHWAY PAPERBACK *Original*

An Archway Paperback published by
POCKET BOOKS, a division of Simon & Schuster Inc.
1230 Avenue of the Americas, New York, NY 10020

Copyright © 1995 by Simon & Schuster Inc.
Produced by Mega-Books, Inc.

ISBN: 0-671-88213-9

First Archway Paperback printing August 1995

10 9 8 7 6 5 4 3 2 1

THE HARDY BOYS, AN ARCHWAY PAPERBACK and colophon are registered trademarks of Simon & Schuster Inc.

THE HARDY BOYS CASEFILES is a trademark of Simon & Schuster Inc.

Cover art by Brian Kotzky

Printed in the U.S.A.

IL 6+

WRONG SIDE OF THE LAW

Chapter

1

SNOW-COVERED EVERGREENS muffled the sound of the snowmobile's powerful engine. Suddenly the rider's two-way radio blasted to life.

"Base to Number One. Urgent! Move out!" a voice crackled. "We see on radar you've got the last enemy agent on your tail."

"Roger," the rider replied. "Moving out." He twisted the throttle of the machine and leaned forward in his seat. A few moments later, as he burst into a clearing, he risked a quick glance over his shoulder and swerved violently to the right. Another snowmobile was just thirty yards behind his. Its rider, face concealed by a dark ski mask, held a stubby assault pistol in one hand. He raised it, aimed, and fired off a short burst. As one slug found its mark, the man being pursued momentarily let go of his right handlebar to grip his left shoulder, then grabbed on again, gritting his teeth against the pain.

A trail opened at the edge of the clearing. The wounded man's eyes widened in recognition as he steered for it. Under the trees the trail curved gently to the left, toward a glimpse of sky. The rider took the curve at full throttle, then, at the last moment, used engine braking to bring the machine almost to a halt. Just over the slight rise dead ahead the trail turned sharply right, along the edge of a forty-foot cliff. The rider leaned into the turn like a motorcycle racer, made it around, and came to a halt a dozen yards farther on. He turned around in his saddle to watch his pursuer.

The man came into sight, his machine throwing up a rooster tail of snow. He must have had the throttle wide open. When he hit the rise, the snowmobile became airborne. In that instant he must have seen the cliff directly ahead. He pushed himself up into a crouch and tried to jump off, but it was too late. He and the snowmobile went sailing off the cliff. A moment later there was a loud crash, then silence.

The survivor unzipped his insulated jumpsuit and bunched a wadded-up handkerchief against his shoulder wound. Then he took a deep breath and clicked the transmit button on his two-way radio.

"This is Number One to base, come in please."

"Base here, reading you loud and clear. Please state your condition."

"The threat has been eliminated. Have sustained a shoulder wound. Will require treatment. Over."

"Congratulations on a job well done, Number One. Return to base immediately for treatment."

The survivor clicked off his radio, put his machine in gear, and drove slowly along the snowy trail as the music came up. The credits appeared on the screen, and the lights in the theater brightened.

"Hey, that was great!" Joe Hardy said. He stood up, stretched, and brushed his blond hair back from his forehead.

His older brother, Frank, stood up, too. "Right," he said with a smile. "Nothing like a chase through the Arctic wilderness to cool you off on a hot summer day. How did you like it, Callie?"

Callie Shaw, Frank's girlfriend, shrugged and said, "It was okay, I guess. The best part was the scenery."

Joe looked at her with disbelief. "The *scenery?*" he exclaimed. "This was supposed to be an adventure flick, not a travelogue."

"I know," Callie said with an apologetic smile. "I just don't think that two hours of people chasing one another and shooting guns is all that much fun. You should know that," she added.

Frank thought about some of the criminal cases he and Joe had helped solve. There were times when they had been chased and shot at, and times when they had chased the bad guys. Exciting times, for sure, but Callie was right. They weren't really what he'd call amusing.

"Hey, let's head over to the food court," Joe suggested after glancing at his watch. "I'm getting the munchies."

Callie laughed. "You get the munchies every hour of the day! What do you do when you and Frank are on a stakeout?"

"I take along lots of candy and chips," Joe replied. "And I keep the cooler in the van filled with sodas. You have to be alert and in top condition to be a good detective, which means eating regularly. That reminds me . . ."

"Okay, okay, let's go!" Frank said, making a show of grabbing Joe by the arm and pulling him out of the theater.

The three took an escalator to the second level of the mall. At the food court, they split up. Frank got two slices of pepperoni pizza and a soda, then looked for a vacant table. Joe joined him, carrying a burrito, two tacos, and a plate of nachos.

A few moments later Callie came to the table with a thick sandwich and a bottle of mineral water. "All right," she said as she sat down. "Real Vermont cheddar, organic vine-ripened tomatoes, avocado, and sprouts, on fresh-baked wheatberry bread. Who could ask for anything more?"

"How about a goat?" Joe suggested.

Callie rolled her eyes and bit into her sandwich. After a few bites she put it down and sighed. "My last day of freedom," she said.

"That's right, you start work tomorrow, don't you?" Joe asked. "Are you looking forward to it?"

Callie sighed. "Not especially," she admitted. "I'm glad I managed to find something, but it's basically clerical work, filing orders for paper plates and napkins. Not exactly glamorous or exciting."

Frank put his hand on top of hers. "Don't worry," he said. "We can still have fun nights and weekends. There'll be trips to the beach, backyard cookouts—"

"And, hopefully, a new mystery to solve?" Callie added with a smile. She turned to Joe.

5

"What about Vanessa? Is she still planning to work on her videos?"

Vanessa Bender, Joe's girlfriend, was practically a professional at creating computer graphics, and she worked out of her mother's animation studio.

Joe nodded. "I guess since she talked to you, she's changed her plans a little. She's going to volunteer with a teen program in town. It's called Hands to Help."

"Oh?" Callie said. "I've heard of them. They work with delinquents, right?"

Joe cleared his throat. "Let's just call them kids with problems," he said. "Family trouble, school problems, as well as problems with the law. The idea is to give them job training and counseling, as well as a place to hang out."

"That sounds like a worthy cause," Frank remarked. "What'll Vanessa be doing?"

"She's going to give workshops on video animation," Joe said. "But everybody in the program acts as a peer counselor, too. So she'll lead a discussion group and counsel some kids. It sounds pretty intense. I hope she'll have a little time and energy left over for me."

"Poor, lonely, abandoned little boy," Callie kidded. "Now you know how Vanessa must feel during football season, when you spend every afternoon and all weekend at practices or games."

When they finished eating, the three wandered through the mall, pausing at a clothing store, where Callie bought a bright yellow tank top. As they passed an electronics store, Joe stopped to admire a notebook computer in the window.

"Hey, Frank," he said. "If we got one of those, we could link it to our computer at home or to the laptop in the van."

"Maybe so, but we couldn't pay for it," Frank replied, pointing out the price tag.

When Joe saw the price, he gulped. "Whoa! Maybe in a year or two," he muttered.

"Don't worry," Frank said cheerfully. "The prices are bound to come down. And meanwhile we can keep records with a notepad and ballpoint, which come to about ninety-seven cents, max."

"That we can handle," Joe told him. "Let's see, anybody remember where we left the van? Which exit do we want?"

"The northeast doors," Callie said. "I spent an hour and a half once walking around looking for my car. Now I make a point of remembering where I parked."

They were just a few feet from the doors when they heard a scream behind them. Had somebody stumbled and fallen down an escalator? All three turned toward the noise.

Without warning a series of shots rang out.

7

The glass door of the Bayport State Bank branch, only a few yards away, shattered into what seemed like a million blue-green fragments.

There were screams from all around now. Shoppers ran in every direction to find a place to take cover.

"Look out!" Frank shouted, grabbing Callie's arm. His pulse was racing as he tugged Callie in the direction of a nearby snack bar. It didn't offer much protection, but anything would be better than standing in the middle of a wide-open corridor.

They hadn't gotten more than three feet when a little knot of bandits in suits, ties, and ski masks burst out of the bank. One of them aimed an assault rifle at the Hardys and Callie, who were caught between them and the exit doors.

"Don't make any dumb moves," he growled. "Against the wall, now!"

Joe and Frank put their hands up and backed toward the wall slowly. Another of the robbers ran over. "Mall security's coming," he blurted out. "They're armed."

"Grab the girl," the first robber ordered. "We'll use her as a shield."

Horrified, Frank watched a second man grab Callie's arm, twist it behind her back, and put a pistol to her head.

"Hey, wait," Frank started to say. The crook with the assault rifle swung around and pointed it directly at Frank's chest.

"No, Frank!" Callie gasped. "Please, do what they say. I'll be all right."

"Good advice. Take it easy, and nobody gets hurt," the man with the rifle said. The others hurried toward the exit doors, with Callie in their midst. Keeping his gun trained on Joe and Frank, the last man backed away. When he reached the doors, he turned and ran.

Chapter

2

FOR AN INSTANT there was dead silence. Then the entire mall erupted in screams and frantic motion. Two security men ran up, pistols in hand. One was shouting into the collar mike of his radio. From inside the bank, a wide-eyed guard ran out, gun in hand, shouting, "Somebody stop them! They just robbed the bank!"

"No, wait! They have a hostage!" Frank shouted back. With Joe right behind him, he ran toward the automatic glass doors. They were just sliding closed, so he shoved his way through an emergency door to the side. At that moment a dark sedan roared away, its tires squealing. Frank had just enough time to catch the first part of the license number before the car screeched around one of the rows of parked cars and vanished.

"Callie!" Frank called. She was sprawled on the sidewalk, dazed. Frank ran over and knelt down next to her.

"It's over," Frank murmured, putting an arm around her shoulders. "They're gone. Are you okay?"

"Frank?" She raised her eyes to his, focusing on him. "Frank, I was so scared! I thought they were going to shoot me. One of them almost did, I think, but the others stopped him."

Callie tried to get up, but fell. Frank took her arm and helped her to her feet. She was still pale and trembling.

From the parking lot entrance came the sound of sirens.

"We'd better get out of the way," Frank said. He and Joe helped Callie to one side, next to a display of lawn furniture and prefabricated metal toolsheds.

Three patrol cars came screaming up and stopped with their hoods pointed toward the mall. The doors were flung open just then. The officers dived out of their cars and took cover behind the open doors, their weapons drawn.

The bank guard who had exchanged shots with the robbers and the two mall security people hurried outside. They held their obviously empty hands in plain sight.

"You're too late," the guard called loudly. "They escaped."

The police officers stood up, holstered their pistols, and moved forward. Frank recognized their old friend, Officer Con Riley. The Hardys knew him from past investigations and also knew he was the most likely member of the department to cooperate with them.

He spotted Joe and Frank almost immediately. "Were you fellows here?" he asked, moving toward them. "Did you see what happened?"

"We were right on the spot," Joe said. "A little too close actually. The robbers took Callie hostage for a couple of minutes."

"Stay here. We'll want statements from the three of you," Riley told them, and took off.

Callie took a ragged breath and said, "I don't feel so good. I could use a glass of water."

"I'll get you one," Joe volunteered, and hurried into the mall. Frank helped Callie to one of the display lawn chairs, where they waited for Joe to return.

After fifteen minutes of questioning witnesses in the bank, Con Riley rejoined them to take their statements. Frank said that he had glimpsed the license plate of the getaway car and gave Riley the fragment he had had time to read. Riley immediately took the two-way radio from his belt and passed along the information to headquarters. "We'll get Motor Vehicles to initiate a computer search right away," he explained. "Now, young lady, what can you tell me about this business?"

Callie told how she'd been grabbed. "I was terrified they'd kidnap me or worse," she said. "But when we got to the car, the guy who seemed to be in charge said to let me go, that I'd just be in the way if they took me along."

"Did you notice anything that might help us ID them?" Riley probed.

Callie frowned, then said, "No, I'm sorry. Afraid not. I wasn't in any shape to notice anything."

Riley's radio buzzed. He picked it up and listened, disappointment showing on his face.

"Well, that's that," he said, replacing the radio. "According to Motor Vehicles, the only match in this part of the state belongs to a silver sports coupe that was reported stolen two weeks ago. Those plates must have been either phony or hot. No surprise there. It's obvious we're dealing with a bunch of pros."

"How's that?" Joe asked. "Have they held up banks before this one?"

Officer Riley nodded. "Seems like it. Last week the South Fork Bank in Orchard Bay was hit. Just like here, the crooks knew how to keep the bank tellers from tripping the silent alarm, they knew which bundles of cash were booby-trapped—"

Callie interrupted. "Booby-trapped cash?" she asked.

"A lot of banks keep special stacks of notes to give to thieves," Frank explained. "They have little bombs hidden inside the stacks that spray indelible dye on whoever's holding them."

"Talk about getting caught red-handed," Joe cracked.

"Well, these guys weren't," Riley pointed out. "They hit each bank right after it got a new shipment of cash. It could just be that they're lucky, of course."

Frank finished the thought. "Or they could have inside information. I wonder . . ."

"Now, hold on," Riley said quickly. "I'm not denying that you boys have helped us a few times. And we're appreciative. But this time, we're dealing with professional thieves. It's a wonder they haven't killed anyone—so far. Tracking them down is the job we're trained and paid to do. It's not for you, no matter how talented you are."

Frank caught Joe's eye and gave a little shake of his head that said, Let me handle this. "We understand, Con. But if we come across a lead, you won't mind if we pass it on to you, will you?"

"Of course not. It's a citizen's duty to help

14

the police bring criminals to justice," he replied, winking broadly at the boys. As he got to his feet, he added, "You have my number. Call me."

Frank stood up, too. "Come on, Callie," he said. "Let's get you home. You must be ready for some quiet time."

After dropping Callie off, Joe and Frank went home. Their aunt Gertrude, who lived with the Hardys, was in the kitchen, slicing peaches and nectarines for a pie. When Joe tried to filch a few slices, she threatened to rap his knuckles with a wooden spoon.

"You'll get your share, once it's cooked," she announced tartly.

Joe grinned. "I'll hold you to that, Aunt Gertrude," he said.

"Is Dad home?" Frank asked.

Aunt Gertrude shook her head. "He had to go to New York City," she said. "A new development in an old case, he told me. He doesn't expect to be back until tomorrow or the next day."

Fenton Hardy was a well-known private detective who was often consulted by police departments around the world.

Frank got two cans of soda from the refrigerator and tossed one to Joe. They carried them into the den.

Joe turned up the air conditioner, then let

himself drop into one of the comfortable armchairs. "Well? What do we do now?" he demanded.

Frank stared down at his hands, then said carefully, "Ordinarily, I might say we let the professionals handle it. But this is different. I've got a personal stake in seeing that the guy who grabbed Callie and held a pistol to her head is put away."

Joe's expression was grim. "I'm with you there. But where do we start?"

"I've been thinking about that," Frank said. "According to Con, the method used in today's stickup was the same one used in a robbery over in Orchard Bay. Both seemed like inside jobs."

"Right," Joe said. "So?"

Frank frowned. "I can see how crooks might get inside information about different branches of the same bank," he said. "But today's stickup was at a branch of Bayport State, and the one last week was at the South Fork Bank."

Joe sat up in his chair. "And didn't Con tell us both stickups happened right after the banks got fresh shipments of cash?"

Frank caught his breath. "That could be the connection!" he exclaimed. "The armored car service! *If* both banks use the same one."

"How do we find out?" Joe asked.

Frank smiled and reached for the phone book. "The biggest armored car company around is Security First," he announced. He called the number in the Yellow Pages and said he was calling for the assistant manager of a Bayport State branch, then called the South Fork Bank and claimed to be the dispatcher for Security First.

When he finished, he gave Joe a thumbs-up sign. "Both banks use Security First," he said. "I think we ought to pay them a visit."

"All right!" Joe said, springing up.

The Security First building was in a small industrial park on the north side of Bayport, not far from the highway. After Joe parked, he and Frank went inside—or tried to. The doors were locked. An armed guard in a Security First uniform eyed them from the other side of an inch-thick bulletproof window.

Over the intercom Frank explained that they had summer research jobs collecting data on the armored car business. Could they interview an official?

The guard wasn't impressed. He picked up his phone and spoke into it for a moment. Then he said, "Sorry, no visitors allowed. You can send a letter."

Frank thought about arguing but decided it was pointless and went back to the van. "Let's keep an eye on the place," Frank suggested as

Joe started the engine. "Maybe we'll think of a way to talk to someone."

Ten minutes later Joe nudged Frank. "Look," he muttered. "There's a guy in a Security First uniform—he just got into that car. Let's follow him."

A quarter of a mile down the road, the guy turned in to the Bayport Diner, went inside, and took a seat at the counter.

The Hardys waited a couple of minutes, then went in. Joe sat next to him as Frank ordered a soda and studied the guard out of the corner of his eye. He was tall and muscular and about twenty-two years old. Something about him was familiar.

Joe made the connection first. "Say," he said. "Didn't you play basketball for Bayport High three or four years back? Wait a minute—Craig Madison, right? You were allstate."

The guard glanced over at him, then turned his attention back to his apple pie. "Yeah, that's right," he muttered.

"I knew I recognized you," Joe continued. "I'm Joe Hardy. This is my brother, Frank. He's a senior at Bayport. We're both on the team."

The guard grunted and kept his eyes on his plate.

Frank leaned across Joe to speak to the

guard. "You're working for Security First? That's the big armored car company, isn't it?"

"Yeah," Joe said, picking up the conversation. "Hey, I heard somebody stuck up the bank at the mall today. Did you hear anything about that?"

The guard stood up, tossed some money on the counter, and left without a word.

"I call that pretty suspicious," Joe said. "He didn't even finish his pie."

"It would be amazing if the first guy we talked to turned out to be working for the thieves," Frank replied. "Did you see how nervous he got the minute you mentioned the holdup? Could be we're onto something."

Joe nodded. "I wonder what we should do next. Hmm—that pie looks good. I think I'll get a piece—can't work on an empty stomach."

Joe was halfway through his pie when Frank noticed two patrol cars pull into the diner parking lot. He smiled to himself. It must be time for their coffee break.

The door to the diner slammed open, and four officers, their guns drawn, rushed in. They spread out, facing Frank and Joe.

"Police. Freeze!" an officer shouted.

Chapter

3

"HANDS FLAT ON THE COUNTER!" one of the men ordered. Another hurried forward and frisked Joe and Frank.

"They're clean, Sarge," he said.

"Okay, now stand up nice and slow,' and put your hands on your heads," the sergeant said.

"But, Sergeant—" Joe started.

"Just do as you're told," the officer said.

"Hey, wait a minute, Sarge," another of his men said. "I think we're making a mistake. These are Fenton Hardy's kids—you know, the detective. They're okay."

"Yeah?" The sergeant tapped Joe on the shoulder. "You. Turn around."

Joe glanced quickly at the nameplates of the

two police officers. "Officer Handke's right, Sergeant Hernandez," he said. "I'm Joe Hardy, and this is my brother, Frank. If you need somebody to vouch for us, you can ask Con Riley or Chief Collig."

"Don't worry, I will," Hernandez said. "But what I want to know is, what were you doing hanging around Security First, then following one of their drivers here and trying to pump him for information? We got a call with a description of you and your van. People who run armored car services are sensitive about strangers who get curious about their business."

Joe glanced over at Frank, who gave a little shrug. "Well, Sergeant," Joe said. "We happened to be at the Bayport Mall today when the bank was held up. We heard a rumor that the crooks might have had inside information, and it occurred to us that somebody with the armored car company might be helping the robberies."

"So you decided to poke around on your own," the sergeant said, slightly angry. "Well, try to understand this. We know our jobs, and we don't need a couple of kids to do them for us. I'm going easy on you this time. But the next time you meddle in police business, I guarantee you'll be in big trouble. Understood?"

"Yes, Sergeant," said Frank. "Understood."

After the police drove off, the counterman, who had been watching from a safe distance, said, "The pie and sodas are on the house. That was better than TV any day."

"Thanks," Frank said, and grinned sheepishly. As they drove home, he told Joe, "I'm thinking that the robbers didn't get their information from someone at the armored car service."

"Why?" Joe asked.

"Look at it this way," Frank said. "If you were a thief who worked for an armored car company, would you hold up a bank with guards and TV monitors and lots of people around? Or would you go for a nice, quiet hijacking of an armored car on a deserted road somewhere?"

"Armored cars are pretty well protected," Joe pointed out.

"Sure. But so are banks," Frank replied. "And in a bank, you're dealing with a lot more people—a lot more things that can go wrong. So why risk it?"

" 'Because that's where the money is'?" Joe suggested, quoting the famous bank robber Willie Sutton.

"Very funny, ha-ha," Frank grumbled. "Anyway, after that warning we just got, we'd better cool it."

Joe pulled over to the curb, stopped the van,

and turned in his seat to stare at Frank. "You mean, give up our investigation?" he asked.

"Of course not," Frank said. "After what happened to Callie, this is a grudge match. But we'll have to be very careful. We don't want the cops any more upset at us than they already are. You know what would be a big help? If Con would lend us a copy of the tape from the bank surveillance cameras. We might spot something the police missed."

Joe put on his turn signal, checked the rearview mirror, and pulled back into traffic. He thought that Con was about as likely to hand over the keys to his squad car, but all he said to Frank was "Hey, it can't hurt to try."

Back home Joe had a message on the answering machine from Vanessa. Would he and Frank like to go out to Hands to Help to meet the director and look around at about five?

Joe dialed and switched on the speakerphone. On the second ring Vanessa answered.

"Joe?" she said. "Somehow I *knew* it was you. You got my message? What about it? I've been having such a really great time at HTH, and I'd love you and Frank to come see what we're doing. You guys could use a little excitement in your lives, right?"

Joe mentally ticked off the day's activities so

far: one bank robbery with abduction, one near-arrest—and it wasn't over yet.

"Yeah," he said, catching Frank's eye. Frank grinned at him. "Sure we do."

"Great," Vanessa said. "Do you want to meet me there, or come by my house first?"

Joe said, "We'll come by for you just before five. We'll go in one car—less air pollution." One of Vanessa's main interests was in protecting the environment.

Joe hung up and passed the phone to Frank so he could call Con Riley.

"Well, well," Riley said. "And what are you boys planning now? Sergeant Hernandez wasn't very happy to meet you this afternoon."

"It was all a misunderstanding," Frank protested.

"It sure was—yours," Riley retorted. "When I told you that chasing down these bandits wasn't a job for you, you somehow thought I didn't mean it. Well, let me be very clear this time. I don't want you to question suspects and investigate this case. Is that understood?"

Frank's jaw tightened. "Those creeps took my girlfriend hostage," he said. "I can't just let that go."

"You're going to have to," Riley told him.

Frank met Joe's gaze. Was he imagining it, or was Con being even tougher than usual?

"Look," Frank said, keeping his voice low

and steady. "Maybe we can still help you from behind the scenes. For example, we could look over the videotapes from the two holdups. With what we saw this afternoon, we might come up with a slightly different point of view. And how much trouble can we get into watching videos?"

Riley laughed. "Frank, you've got enough nerve for three people. Those videos are official evidence, and you know it. I can't give out a copy of them."

"I understand," Frank said glumly. "Okay, Con. If we come across anything that might be helpful, we'll let you know."

He hung up.

Joe eyed him incredulously. "We're giving up?" he demanded.

"Not a chance," Frank replied. "But I don't think the direct approach is going to get us very far. We have to come up with something else."

As they drove across town to the former elementary school that housed Hands to Help, Vanessa told Joe and Frank more about the program.

"First of all, these kids need to learn technical skills that'll help them find jobs," she explained. "That's why I'm giving my courses in video production and animation, for example.

25

There's a lot of demand for people with those skills. But skills aren't enough. These kids need to have confidence and a sense of pride in themselves, too."

"That's where the counseling comes in, right?" Frank asked.

Vanessa nodded. "Part of it's really practical, like how to dress for a job interview and what to say. But the kids in the program get psychological support, too. Everyone *expects* them to succeed, and that helps make it happen for them. For a lot of kids, this is the first time they've known anyone who believed in them."

"I get it," Joe said, "but I'm fuzzy on the details. How old are these kids?"

"The youngest are twelve or so, and the oldest are sixteen or seventeen," Vanessa answered. "It's a little weird getting used to being a counselor to somebody who's the same age as I am. But this peer model business works, I'm told."

"Do the kids live at HTH?" Joe asked.

"If their home situations are bad, they can live at HTH," Vanessa said. "During the school year, the program is just evenings and weekends. In the summer, we manage to keep the kids busy almost full-time."

"Let's say I'm a kid who's just coming into

the program," Joe continued. "What happens first?"

"First? Well, you have a meeting with Pat—that's Pat McMillan, the director. He checks out your talents, your problems, your interests, your family situation—all that. Then you and he work out a kind of contract. What kind of job you'll get, what progress you intend to make—things like that."

"Job?" Frank asked.

"Sure. Pat manages to find part-time jobs for everyone," Vanessa told him. "It's important for their self-images, and they make some money, too.

"I'm making it all sound so serious. We have a lot of fun, too. HTH is like a community center," Vanessa added. "There's a really active sports program, and some of the kids have formed a rock group. Here we are."

Joe pulled into the driveway and parked near the basketball court. A game was going on. Vanessa and the Hardys went over to watch.

A tall, muscular guy with red hair took a pass and made a quick move for the basket. He was going in for a layup when he stumbled over a young kid with freckles and stringy blond hair. The big guy with red hair fell hard and clutched his knee. Then he sprang up, shouting, "You tripped me, Ricky! I'm going to wipe the court with you!"

"Hey, hold on, Gil," one of Gil's teammates said. "He didn't mean it."

Gil paid no attention. He made a lunge at Ricky, who started to run away. Gil was right behind him. Ricky ran straight at the Hardys, grabbed Joe's elbow, and whipped around to hide behind him. Gil tried to dodge around Joe to grab the kid.

"Just a second," Joe said as the other players hurried over. "Take a deep breath, buddy. That sure looked like an accident to me."

"Butt out, turkey," Gil growled. He made a sudden move to one side, but Ricky managed to keep Joe between himself and his attacker.

Gil gave Joe's shoulder a shove. Joe absorbed the blow and stayed where he was. "Listen, friend," he said in a warning tone. "I think you'd better just chill out. Or if you have to pick on somebody, maybe you should find somebody your own size."

Gil's face turned almost as red as his hair. He planted his feet solidly, pivoted at the waist, and threw a hard right, straight at Joe's midsection.

Chapter

4

WHEN FRANK SAW GIL heating up, he was ready to jump in. Gil looked pretty tough, and so did a lot of the others on the court. If some of them joined in and ganged up on Joe, he could be in a major brawl.

Gil's punch was aimed straight at Joe's solar plexus, but Joe took a quick step to his left and clamped his right hand down on Gil's wrist. He brought his left hand up under Gil's elbow and let the attacker's own momentum twist his arm into a hammerlock.

"Ow!" Gil hollered, and fell to his knees. "I won't forget this, turkey. Let go of me, or you'll be sorry!"

"I'll let go as soon as you calm down," Joe said. "How about it?"

In response, Gil slammed Joe in the calf with his left fist.

Joe grunted with pain, then said, "Now, now. Let's make nice." He gave Gil's right wrist a little extra twist.

"Hey, what's going on here?" someone shouted in a deep voice.

Frank looked around. A big, burly guy with a graying beard and a receding hairline was moving quickly toward them.

Ricky said, "Nothing, Pat. It's okay."

"Come on, what happened?" Pat demanded of the other players.

One of them, with a scar on his cheek, stepped forward. "Gil lost it after he tripped over Ricky," he reported. "He said he was going to stomp Ricky. But this guy got in the way, so Gil threw a punch at him."

Another player, tall and skinny, took up the story. "Then the blond dude threw some kind of trick hold on Gil and stopped him cold."

Pat nodded at Joe. "Let him go," he said. "I'll take over now."

Joe released Gil's wrist and took a quick step back—just in case. All Gil did was get to his feet, rub his elbow, and bend over to brush the dirt off his knees. He took a long time retying his high-tops, which were laced in a complicated pattern that looked like a ladder running up the front of the shoe. Frank couldn't recall seeing it before, but glancing around, he noticed that several other players had their sneakers laced the same way. He smiled to himself. Chances were, by fall, everyone at Bayport High would be doing it—himself and Joe included.

"Well, Gil?" Pat said. "What do *you* think happened?"

"I lost my temper," Gil said in an undertone. "But I still think Ricky tripped me."

"I didn't!" the blond kid declared loudly. "It was an accident!"

"What's that kind of accident called in basketball, Ricky?" Pat asked in a mild voice.

Ricky stared at the tips of his sneakers. "It's called a foul," he said.

"Then you made a mistake, right?" Pat said. Ricky nodded. "And then Gil, instead of following the rules, made his own mistake. Right, Gil?"

"Right," Gil muttered.

Pat paused for a moment, then said, "Okay, I want you two to shake hands and get back to the game. We'll overlook the foul this time, Ricky, but try not to let it happen again."

"Hey, what about my foul shot?" Gil demanded.

31

Joe broke in. "You already took your foul shot," he said with a grin. "At me!"

For a moment Gil glared at Joe. Then he gave a little laugh and said, "Yeah, I guess I did." He turned to Ricky and stuck out his hand. Ricky hesitated for a moment, then shook it. The two of them walked back onto the court, the others trailing after them.

Pat gave a loud sigh. "If only it were always that easy," he said. "Vanessa, am I right that these are the friends you were telling me about? The detectives?"

"That's right." Vanessa introduced Joe and Frank, who shook hands with Pat.

"You had quite an introduction to our bunch," Pat said with an infectious smile. "Don't worry, it's not always this lively. Come on inside. I'll give you some background on what we're doing, then we can take a look around."

Pat's office looked as if it had once been the supply closet when the building had been a school. He edged past his desk and sat down, then waved the Hardys to two folding chairs. Vanessa moved a stack of papers to the floor and perched on the radiator cover.

Pat folded his hands on the desk in front of him and said, "Well, let me start by giving you a little personal history. When I was fifteen, I used to hang out with a pretty tough bunch of kids. Of course, I eventually got in trouble with the law—grand theft auto, to be exact. Some of my buddies got into even deeper trouble. A few of them ended up dead, or locked up for life. But I was lucky. A friend of my dad's was a youth counselor, and he took charge of me. I didn't make it easy for him, and I *know* he didn't make it easy on me. But in time he straightened me out. I finished high school, went to college, got a degree in psychology, and went to graduate school. After a few years in private practice, I realized that what I really wanted to do was use my training and skills to help teens who were headed for trouble."

"Pat started Hands to Help by himself," Vanessa said proudly.

Pat smiled. "Well, not really, Vanessa. I had the original idea, but I never could have gotten anywhere without a lot of help. It's volunteers who keep the program going and growing."

"Where do the kids in the program come from?" Frank asked. "Is it a neighborhood-based organization?"

"Not at all," Pat replied, shaking his head. "Our members come from all over Bayport and the surrounding area. Some are referred to us by juvenile courts or social agencies. But more and more come through word of mouth. Friends bring friends."

He paused and looked down at his hands,

then said, "Vanessa tells me that you're both fine athletes, as well as having a lot of other impressive skills. You strike me as being exactly the kind of role models our members need. Have you ever thought about volunteering some time to a program like ours? You could make a real difference."

Frank had seen the question coming, but didn't know how to answer it. Ordinarily, he would have said yes right away, but he felt a personal commitment to work on the bank robberies.

He glanced over at Joe, who seemed to be just as uncertain, probably for the same reason.

"How about this?" Pat continued. "Give us a week or so. Then, after you've gotten a real feel for what we're doing, if you want to continue, terrific. If you don't, that's okay, too. What do you say?"

Frank felt under a lot of pressure. Vanessa was watching him and Joe expectantly. Could he and Joe give some time to the program and still follow up on their investigation?

Pat broke in on Frank's thoughts, saying, "Don't give me your answer now. Have a look around first. I think you'll like what you see and want to lend a hand."

They followed Pat down the hall and stopped at a classroom door to peek in. Then he quietly opened the door and motioned for them to follow him in. Half a dozen teens were working at computers. The way most of them were dressed, in baggy jeans, huge oversize T-shirts, and high-tops with woolly laces, made them look like members of a street gang rather than a computer class. One guy gave Frank and Joe a challenging look, as if they were trespassing on his turf. Then he noticed Pat and Vanessa and went back to his computer.

The instructor, a young woman who looked like a college student, smiled at them. "Oh, hi, Pat. Hi, Vanessa," she said. Some of the teens smiled and said hi as well.

Pat introduced Joe and Frank to the class and to the instructor, whose name was Gail. He explained that the brothers were thinking about becoming volunteers.

"Welcome," Gail said. "This, as you see, is a computer literacy workshop. We're learning about word processing, and then we'll take a look at spreadsheets and databases. Then it starts getting *really* complicated—flow charts, critical path techniques, stuff like that."

There were scattered boos and groans from the participants. Gail wrinkled her nose at them.

"You seem to be really well equipped," Frank remarked, noticing the flatbed scanner, two laser printers, and a color ink-jet printer.

"We have Pat to thank for that," Gail said. "The world's best scrounger."

Pat said, "Practically everything you see was donated by companies that were upgrading their systems. It's not the very latest, but it's more than powerful enough for us.

"Thanks, Gail. We'll let you get back to what you're doing," she added.

Farther down the hall a man in his thirties was leading a workshop in troubleshooting electronic equipment. He was about five-ten, with dark hair, dark shadows under his eyes, and the beginnings of a potbelly. His sharply creased gray pants, white shirt, and embroidered suspenders struck Frank as being somehow out of place.

Pat introduced him as Jack Nevins. "Jack's the founder and president of Nevatronics, Inc.," he added. "You've probably noticed their plant near the train station. Jack was one of the first people to get behind Hands to Help, not just with money, but with his time."

Nevins gave a brief smile. "It's a privilege for me to volunteer."

Frank looked over at Joe and raised one eyebrow. His brother seemed to share the feeling that either all the volunteers were incredibly dedicated, or they had all memorized the same lines.

Next Pat led the way to the Arts and Crafts

room. Frank stayed behind to take a closer look at some of the electronic test equipment the kids in Jack's workshop were using. When he went out into the hallway, he didn't see the others.

Frank decided to go right. He had taken only a few steps when he heard someone say, in a voice full of menace, "You better decide, turkey, and do it fast. If you're not with us, you're against us. And if you're against us, you could get hurt."

Chapter

5

THE THREATENING WORDS had come from inside the next classroom. For one moment Frank wondered if someone might be rehearsing a play. He quickly dismissed the idea.

Another voice murmured something Frank couldn't make out.

"You heard me," the first voice growled. "Make up your mind. Do you want it easy, or hard?"

Footsteps approached the open door of the classroom. Frank glanced around and backed into an alcove, where he flattened himself against the wall. The footsteps moved out of the room and turned away from him. He risked a quick look. He thought he'd recognized that voice. One of the people who was walking away was the tall redheaded kid, Gil, who had thrown a punch at Joe. The other guy was shorter and stocky, with long black hair. Frank caught a glimpse of a gold hoop earring in his left ear.

Frank waited until they turned a corner, then he set off in search of Pat, Joe, and Vanessa. A girl in a red tank top gave him directions to the Arts and Crafts room. The others were still there, looking over some of the crafts projects the kids were working on.

"Hey, Frank, we thought we'd lost you," Pat said. "We were getting ready to send out a St. Bernard dog."

"Sorry," Frank replied. "First I got distracted, then I got lost. Luckily, someone told me where to go. A guy with black hair and a gold earring."

"That sounds like Vinnie Alessandro," Pat said. "I'm glad he was helpful. When he first joined the program a couple of months ago, he was pretty resentful."

As they left the workshop, Pat asked, "Well? What do you think?"

Joe looked over at Frank and raised an eyebrow. Frank wanted to have a relaxing summer vacation, with no obligations, but he quickly put his dream aside and gave a nod to Joe.

"We'd like to give it a try, Pat. It looks like a really worthwhile program."

"I was hoping you'd say that," Pat replied. "Now, what I suggest is that you start off as peer counselors, and if you like, you could also help out with one activity that interests you."

"Do you need someone to help coach basketball?" Joe asked.

"You're on," Pat said. "How about you, Frank?"

"I know something about martial arts," Frank said.

Pat clapped him on the shoulder. "Great. I'll tell Lisa Tang, our karate coach, to expect you. Come on back to my office, and I'll put together a schedule for you. Oh, yes—and we're having an excursion to the beach tomorrow afternoon. I hope you can join us."

On the way back to Vanessa's house, Frank related what he'd overheard in the hallway. "What I'm wondering," he concluded, "is, who's this 'us' Gil was talking about? And why was he telling the other guy that he'd get hurt if he wasn't with whoever 'us' is? Any ideas, Vanessa?"

Vanessa shook her head. "Not really, Frank," she said. "I've noticed that Gil has a lot of influence over the other kids in the program. But I can't imagine why he'd be threatening Vinnie."

Frank frowned. "How about this?" he said to Vanessa. "From what you say, a lot of the kids in the program have already had brushes with the law, and the first thing we saw when we got here was a fight. Then the minute I was alone, I heard a serious threat. I've got to wonder if Gil is putting together a gang from members of Hands to Help."

"I haven't noticed anything like that," Vanessa said. She sounded troubled. "I'll tell you, though—I'll keep my eyes and ears open."

"So will we," Frank said with a laugh. "Don't forget tomorrow morning Joe and I are part of the program, too."

The next morning the Hardys made their way through rush-hour traffic toward HTH. Joe was at the wheel. Frank picked up their cellular phone and punched in Con Riley's number.

"Yeah, Riley here," a familiar voice said.

Frank identified himself, then asked, "Has anything new turned up on those bank robbers?"

"So far, nothing," Riley replied. "But I should tell you, we went over the personnel files of the Security First armored car company with a fine-tooth comb. They're clean. Nice try, boys, but no cigar."

"How about the surveillance cameras?" Frank asked. "Anything significant there?"

Riley laughed. "Just a bank robbery in progress. Four thieves with ski masks and guns, and a lot of frightened civilians. Just like on TV."

Frank said, "You said you'd think about letting us see the tapes."

"I wouldn't hold my breath if I were you," Riley told him. "We're running a police department here. I know you, boys. If you did notice something, you wouldn't be able to resist following up on it yourselves. And after yesterday afternoon, I don't need to remind you how we feel about amateur detectives here in the department."

Frank bit back his comment. What was the point of getting their best friend on the Bayport force mad at them? "Okay, thanks, Officer Riley," he said.

He replaced the phone and turned to Joe. "Nothing new," he reported. "You know, I've been thinking, maybe the robbers don't *need* to have inside information. What I mean is this. Anyone who ever worked in a bank is going to know about silent alarms and booby-trapped bundles of bills. Hey, you can even find out a lot of that stuff by reading magazine articles. And you can figure out the schedule for cash deliveries if you're willing to keep an eye on a bank long enough."

"I see your point," Joe said. "Then you think we're at a dead end?"

Frank hesitated. "Well, not quite," he said. "There are the videos. And if the gang sticks up another bank—and I guess they will—they might make a mistake."

"They already did," Joe said, grinning. "They tried to grab your girlfriend as a hostage. And you're not going to forgive and forget that."

They parked the van in the lot outside the former elementary school. As they went up the walk, Pat appeared in the doorway, a smile on his face.

"Welcome," he called. "Everybody's looking forward to working with you fellows. Come along, I'll show you around."

As he led them down the corridor, Pat continued, "Joe, you've got basketball clinic at eleven. How does that sound?"

"Great," Joe responded, glancing at his watch.

"In the meantime," Pat added, "I want you to sit in on one of our discussion groups to get the feel of them. There's one that's just starting on jobs and careers."

"Um—fine," Joe said.

Pat stopped at a classroom door and opened it. Inside, a dozen teens were sitting in a circle. They all turned to look at the door.

43

Joe glanced at Frank and rolled his eyes. Then he walked into the room and said, "Hi. I'm Joe Hardy."

Pat smiled and motioned for Frank to continue down the corridor.

"Now let's go to the gym," he said to Frank. "Lisa Tang is expecting you this morning, so feel free to jump right into her class."

They found Lisa talking to eight or ten kids sitting in a row on the mats. The group was about half boys, half girls, and ranged in age from early to midteens. Lisa was about twenty, with short black hair and an attractive, oval-shaped face. Slim and no more than five-four, she moved gracefully. She nodded to Pat and Frank without interrupting her story.

"One of the most effective methods is called the White Crane style of kung fu," she said. "It was developed in China many hundreds of years ago. The crane is a bird with long legs, wide wings, and a long beak, but it doesn't have much strength. To defend itself, it must move in close enough to strike with its wings or beak, then back away before the opponent can counterattack. I will show you."

She beckoned to Frank. He slipped off his shoes and socks and joined her on the mat. They bowed to each other, then Lisa said, "This is Frank, who will also be teaching you. Frank, please attack me."

Frank put his right leg slightly forward and shifted his weight to the left. His hands were together, just below his waist. Suddenly he swung them to the left and up, in a semicircular sweep that ended with a right hand-sword strike at Lisa's collarbone.

It never connected. The moment he began to move, Lisa made a lightning hop to her right, raising her left arm to divert his blow. His hand slipped harmlessly past her. Instantly she grabbed his shirt in both fists and pulled him forward to butt him in the nose with her forehead. She hit him just hard enough for him to feel it, then jumped back out of his reach. Putting her hands on her thighs, she gave him another bow. He returned it, a little irritated that she had handled him so effortlessly. He also felt admiration for Lisa's superior skills. He might be helping to teach this workshop, but he had a hunch he was going to learn a few things, too.

"Any questions?" Lisa asked. "None? Okay, then we can start. Form two lines, an arm's length from your neighbor. We'll begin with exercises to get the *chi*, or energy, flowing in your bodies. . . ."

Joe's discussion group let out just before eleven, and he went straight to the locker room to change into his basketball shorts. He was still thinking over some of the comments the kids in the group had made about dead-end jobs flipping hamburgers. Could HTH really make a difference for them? He hoped so.

Gradually he began to be aware of a conversation on the other side of the bank of lockers.

"I know I've got to protect myself," one guy was saying. "I'm not about to let some dude walk all over me. But a piece?"

"It's up to you," the other guy told him. "You don't want to pack one, fine. But if you do, I'll tell you what to do. Just go to Fifth and Main at seven tonight and look for a van, about five years old, with Virginia plates."

"I'm not saying I'll do it," the first guy said. "But if I do, I'm not going to want to settle for a popgun. If you want respect, you got to show some real firepower, right?"

The other guy gave a snort. "Listen," he said, as they walked out the door. "If you got the cash, you can walk away with anything from a Streetsweeper shotgun to a MAC-10 submachine gun."

Chapter

6

MACHINE GUNS being sold on the streets of Bayport? This was urgent. Joe finished tying his shoelaces and walked swiftly toward the door. Just as he reached it, it swung open and three guys started in. By the time Joe edged past them, the hallway outside was empty. The two guys had gotten away.

Joe stopped in the middle of the hall, his hands on his hips, and looked both ways. What had those two been doing in the locker room? Changing, obviously. But out of athletic clothes, or into them? Would he find them waiting for him on the basketball court? If he did, how would he know who they were?

Joe let out a grunt of frustration and went outside. Half a dozen players were clustered around each end of the court, practicing layups and rebounding. Joe stood on the sidelines and watched, taking mental notes on the players. Some were obviously beginners, but there were four or five who moved and handled the ball well. One was Gil, the guy with red hair who had tried to start a fight with Joe. Ricky, the kid Gil had been picking on, was out there, too, making up for his lack of height with sheer energy.

Had any of these guys been in the locker room a few minutes before? Most of them had damp sweat patches on their T-shirts, which meant they'd been playing for at least a few minutes. Still, it was a warm day. Anyone who was running around would break a sweat pretty quickly.

Joe shook his head and decided that it was time to start doing what he was there to do. He walked out onto the court, corralled four of the beginners, and got them into a circle to practice passing. As soon as they had the routine down, he moved over to the far basket and worked with some of the more skilled players on rebounding. Whenever he glanced around, he saw Gil glaring at him from the other end of the court. He shrugged it off. The guy obviously had an attitude problem.

Joe was watching one kid go up for a layup when someone tapped him on the shoulder.

"What do you say to some one-on-one?" Gil said. "If you're up to it, that is."

Joe gave him a cold smile. "You got it," he said. He snapped his fingers, and one of the guys he'd been coaching tossed him a ball. Joe bounced it once, feinted to the left, and went right. Gil was all over him. Joe circled, his back to the basket, until he was nearly out of bounds, then uncoiled like a spring with a turn-around jump shot. *Swish!*

Gil took the ball with a sour look. As he drove toward the basket, his elbow made its own drive—right at Joe's stomach. Joe moved back just in time.

Gil took his shot and missed but managed to outjump Joe for the rebound—with some unofficial help from his knee. His tip-in circled the rim a couple of times and dropped through.

"One all. Go, Joe!" Ricky called from the sidelines. Gil was furious. Joe took advantage of this distraction to dodge under Gil's outstretched arm and sink another. Total game time, about fifteen seconds. Joe wiped his face with the tail of his T-shirt and gave Gil a big grin. He got a mean scowl in return.

After that Joe spent more energy dodging Gil's shoulders, elbows, knees, and feet than on trying to make baskets. A couple of times

Gil was wide-open to being fouled, and Joe was really tempted to give him some of his own medicine. Then he remembered that the people he was supposed to be coaching were watching every move he made. What kind of example would that be?

The score stood at four to three when Joe beat Gil to the rebound on a missed shot. As he landed, his elbow caught Gil just under the ear. Gil went down, clutching his neck and groaning loudly. Joe knew it had been an accident. He also knew that his chances of convincing Gil of that were nonexistent. Guys who played dirty liked to think that everybody else played just as dirty.

"Hey, I'm sorry, man," Joe said. "It was an accident. Here, let me help you up."

He stretched out a hand. Gil swatted it away. "Get away from me," he growled. "I'll settle with you later." He clambered to his feet and walked away, muttering to himself. Joe watched him for a moment, then shrugged and returned to his coaching duties.

At lunchtime Frank and Joe drove to a nearby pizzeria. Joe recounted the conversation he had overheard in the dressing room that morning.

Frank looked at him in shock and disbelief. "Kids buying high-powered weapons, right here in Bayport?" he exclaimed. "That's awful! We've got to do something. We'll check it out, then pass it on to the authorities."

"This on top of tracking down the hoods who grabbed Callie," Joe muttered.

"We've got a lot of balls in the air," Frank said. "Speaking of which, how did your coaching go?"

"Okay," Joe replied shortly. He didn't feel like telling Frank about his bout with Gil quite yet. Sometimes Frank was too quick to take Joe's side in a dispute, which made it harder for Joe to arrive at a compromise. "How about your karate workshop?"

Frank grinned. "First of all, it's more kung fu than karate," he said. "The instructor's name is Lisa, and she's really good. In a match, I think my size and reach might give me the edge, but I wouldn't bet on it."

"That good, huh?" Joe replied. "I'd like to watch her in action. What school of kung fu, Long Fist?"

"Mostly White Crane," Frank told him. "I had a soda with her after the class. She wants to start her own martial-arts school someday. She offered me a job as an instructor."

"Great, but I wouldn't start spending my salary yet if I were you," Joe said dryly. "Which reminds me—how'd you like to treat me to another slice of pizza? I left my money in my other pants."

When the Hardys got back to Hands to Help, there was a crowd in front of the building. Everyone was ready for the afternoon excursion to the beach. Their van was to be part of a convoy of two other vans and a car. Vanessa spotted them and came over with an equipment bag on her shoulder. She slung it behind the backseat, then went back and returned with four kids. One of them was Ricky, who flashed Joe a big grin as he climbed in.

"Hey, that was neat the way you handled Gil," Ricky said.

Frank looked back. "What did he do?" he asked curiously.

Ricky grinned. "He really cleaned his clock. First he took him on, one-on-one, and outshot him. Then he decked him."

Joe stared straight ahead. He could sense Frank's gaze on him. His face grew warm. "Hey, that was an accident," he said.

"Yeah, right," Ricky said. "Whatever you say, Joe."

Pat got the rest of the group together, and they set off on the twenty-minute drive to the state park. Just before they got onto the parkway, they passed the branch of the South Fork Bank that had been held up. Joe glanced over at Frank and saw that he, too, had noticed.

"Wow, a day at the beach," a girl named Alison said. "I used to go all the time, when my dad was around."

The guy next to her asked, "What happened? Did he die?"

"No, he got laid off and went off to California to look for work," Alison replied. "He said he'd send for us as soon as he was settled. But that was four years ago."

"Huh! If you had *my* dad, you'd be glad to see him go," a talkative girl named Maria said. "He gets mad at me every time I open my mouth."

Ricky laughed and said, "You mean you shut it sometimes? That's news!"

While the others laughed, Maria aimed a mock punch at Ricky, who pretended to hide behind Vanessa.

"Hey, leave me out of this!" Vanessa said. "Look, we're almost there."

Pat had reserved a picnic area on a wooded bluff overlooking the bay of the ocean. Two staff members stayed there to unpack the supplies and start a charcoal fire in the barbecue pit. Everyone else headed for the changing room to put on their suits, then made a dash down to the beach.

"Joe?" Vanessa said. "Would you help me set up a volleyball net?"

She emptied the equipment bag on the sand.

It contained a net, two telescoping poles, and a supply of tent stakes, as well as a volleyball, a basketball, and three Frisbees. Joe tossed the Frisbees to some of the kids on the beach, then set to work. He hammered the poles into the sand, then supported them with guylines while Vanessa attached the net. It was hot work. By the time they were done, Vanessa and Joe were more than ready for a swim.

"Race you to the water," Vanessa said with an impish grin.

Joe shook his head. "I'm already too hot," he groaned. He stepped past her and moved in front, blocking her, then said, "Okay, *go!*"

"Cheater!" Vanessa shouted as she ran down the beach after him. Just as Joe ran into the water, she flashed past him in a shallow dive, then surfaced and splashed him. "I won," she announced.

Joe in turn dived into an oncoming wave. Once underwater, out of sight, he circled quickly around. Two powerful strokes brought him back to where Vanessa was standing in waist-deep water. He gripped one of her ankles and tugged. She fell sideways with an indignant shout and a mighty splash.

"Okay, truce," she spluttered, regaining her feet. She ducked, as a basketball whizzed by her head.

"Sorry, Vanessa," someone called.

Joe looked around. Six or eight kids were in a circle, chest-deep in the surf, tossing the basketball around. The kids all acted tense. Some were glaring, others acted nervous. Joe felt a fight could break out at any minute and started toward them, ready to intervene.

"Hey, Vinnie," one of the kids shouted. "Catch."

The ball sailed across the circle to a guy with long black hair and an earring. He caught it and instantly hurled it in the direction of Gil. It hit an incoming wave just short of Gil and splashed water in his face.

Reddening, Gil seized the ball and flung it right back as hard as he could. As he threw, he shouted, "Yours, Vinnie!"

The basketball hit the water about two feet in front of Vinnie and ricocheted upward, hitting him hard just under the point of his chin. Vinnie fell backward and slumped down under the water.

Chapter

7

JOE FROZE when the basketball hit Vinnie. Something about the way Vinnie's head snapped back told him this was an emergency. As Vinnie slipped out of sight under the waves, Joe launched himself toward him. A small part of his mind noted that so far he was the only one who was alarmed. Everyone else apparently thought Vinnie was horsing around.

A dozen fast strokes brought Joe to where Vinnie had been. He put his feet down and stood up. The water came to just above his waist. Narrowing his eyes against the glare of sunlight reflecting off the water, he quickly scanned the area. There!

Vinnie was floating facedown, just below the

surface. Joe grabbed him under the arms and pulled his head up out of the water. Then he wrestled the limp body up onto his shoulders in a firefighter's carry. A clamor of voices broke out around him, but Joe ignored them. All he could think about was getting the unconscious boy to the beach, checking his condition, and starting to administer CPR, if necessary.

By the time Joe reached the edge of the surf, Frank and Pat had rushed over to help him. Together, they lowered Vinnie to the sand. Frank got on hands and knees and leaned over to put his ear near Vinnie's mouth. At that moment Vinnie began to cough violently. Frank gave a relieved nod.

"He's okay, I think," Frank said.

There was a gasp of relief from the crowd.

"Okay, everybody," Pat said, raising his voice. "Back off and give us some room."

Vinnie opened his eyes, took a deep breath, and struggled to sit up. Frank and Joe helped him.

"My chest hurts," he whispered hoarsely. "My throat, too. And my chin. Who punched me?"

"Just take it easy for a few minutes," Joe said. "You'll be all right."

Vinnie looked around at the circle of concerned faces. "Now I remember," he said. "We were playing catch in the water. Gil threw the ball and hit me in the face."

"It was an accident," Gil said loudly. He grabbed Pat's arm and repeated, "An accident, that's all. I wasn't aiming to hit him, really I wasn't."

"Okay, Gil, we understand," Pat said. "Nobody's blaming you."

Frank wasn't so sure. Only that morning he had overheard Gil threatening Vinnie. And now, because of Gil, Vinnie had almost drowned. A coincidence? It was possible, but Frank was still considering the other possibility—that something shady was going on at Hands to Help, and that Gil was right in the middle of it. In that case he might have deliberately tried to hit Vinnie. He couldn't have known that the blow would be so deadly. Even if he had only been trying to frighten or intimidate Vinnie, it would be a good idea to keep a close watch on him. His next target might be Ricky, or even Joe or Frank.

With Joe's help, Vinnie stumbled to his feet. "I've got to get out of the sun," he murmured. "It's making me dizzy."

"Come on. I'll take you up the hill," Joe replied. "You can sit in the shade."

As the two walked slowly toward the wooden stairs, Pat said, "Okay, everybody.

Emergency's over. Let's all get back to having a good time. A good, *safe* time."

The crowd slowly dispersed. Frank noticed that the kids all avoided Gil, who wore an angry, resentful expression. After a couple of minutes he jogged down the beach to dive into the water by himself.

Frank picked up a Frisbee and tossed it to Vanessa. She caught it, glanced around, and called out, "Hey, Juanita—want to play?" Before long, the bright red disk was sailing back and forth across the beach.

"Frank?" Pat said a while later. "How about you and Vanessa choose sides for volleyball? Winners get to eat first."

"Nothing better than a hot dog grilled over a charcoal fire," Joe said to Vanessa between bites.

Vanessa replied, "Oh? How about a charbroiled burger with loads of pickles and onions?"

In response, Joe turned his head away and held his nose.

"Listen, buster," Vanessa said, "if I hadn't picked you for my volleyball team, you'd still be back there in line with your poor, hungry brother."

"Ha!" Joe retorted. "If you hadn't picked

59

me, you'd still be in line. Who made that spike for the winning point?"

"And who set you up, Mister Prima Donna?" Vanessa demanded.

From his place in line, Frank called, "Teamwork, boys and girls. That's what wins the game. Say, Joe, if you're too busy to eat that frank, it *does* have my name on it, you know."

Everyone within earshot booed Frank's corny joke. He responded by taking an elaborate bow. Both brothers were glad to see that the shock of Vinnie's near-disaster had worn off. Vinnie himself seemed to be having as much fun as anyone, though an ugly bruise was developing on his chin.

The only person who was obviously not having a good time was Gil. He hung back by himself. Did he still think they were blaming him for nearly drowning Vinnie? The way he was acting wouldn't stop anybody's suspicions. Frank considered trying to bring him into the party. He hesitated because he still wondered if Gil's throw had been meant to harm Vinnie. If so, it wouldn't hurt Gil to realize that this sort of behavior could have unpleasant consequences.

Frank finally reached the serving table. He took both a burger and a hot dog, added a big handful of chips, and with both hands carefully balanced a can of soda on top. Lisa was at one of the tables, with some kids Frank recognized from her morning class. Frank joined them. They were talking about the pluses and minuses of different martial arts. He listened as he ate, then put in a modest plug for his own favorite, aikido. They made him promise to give them a demonstration at their next workshop.

After eating, everybody helped clean up and pack up the vans for the return trip. Frank and Joe helped with the unloading and cleanup back at HTH, then said their goodbye for the day.

Even with a stop at a take-out store for sandwiches and sodas, they reached the corner of Fifth and Main, where they expected to find the gun smugglers, by six forty-five that evening. Joe parked the van two cars in from the corner. Then he and Frank moved into the back to wait and watch.

The neighborhood had been nice once, but that was a long time ago. On one corner was a six-story apartment building, constructed with a courtyard and reflecting pool in front. Now an old, charred mattress half-filled the dried-up pool, and most of the windows in the building were boarded over. Four guys were standing together near the building entrance, watching the street with empty eyes.

"Some reception committee," Joe commented. "Guaranteed to make you feel right at home."

Frank tapped his arm. "Look," he said quietly. A battered white Wanderer model van had just pulled up to the curb diagonally across the intersection. It was streaked with road dirt. The wipers had made two pie-shaped clear spaces on the filthy windshield. Frank reached behind him for a pair of small but powerful binoculars and brought them to his eyes. "Virginia plates," he reported, unable to read the exact numbers. "Hey, look," he said.

One of the men who had been holding up the wall of the building across the way walked slowly over to the van. The van blocked Frank and Joe's view of whatever he was doing. But as he returned to his friends, Frank noticed that he was now wearing the tails of his shirt out. Hiding something, such as a handgun?

Over the next twenty minutes three other people approached the van; each spent a few minutes and then left. One came on foot, another on a motorcycle, and the third, a guy in his midtwenties, arrived in a flashy sports car. Joe snapped pictures of each of them, but the Hardys still hadn't got a glimpse of whoever was inside the van.

Finally Joe said, "I'm going over there."

Frank said, "That's not a very good idea. If

we really are dealing with a gun smuggler, he could be dangerous—and armed."

"I'll be careful," Joe replied. "How are they going to know I'm not just another customer? Besides, if these creeps are selling guns to everybody in town including the kids from HTH, it's worth taking some risks to stop them."

Joe slipped out of the side door and walked away from the corner. Halfway down the block, he crossed the street and returned on the other side. As he approached the van, he saw that the curbside door was open. His pulse started racing. He swallowed and wiped his damp palms on the legs of his jeans. Then he took a deep breath and stepped forward. A man with long blond hair and a bushy blond mustache was inside the van, sitting in a swiveling captain's chair with a newspaper open on his lap. He eyed Joe coldly.

"Er, hi," Joe said, stopping by the open door. "I heard I could get some protection here. Is that right?"

The man put his hand under the newspaper. When he brought it out again, he was holding an automatic pistol. "This kind of protection?" he said. He pointed the pistol at Joe's chest and added, "Get inside and shut the door. Make it fast."

Chapter

8

JOE HESITATED. Get into the van with an armed stranger? He would have no chance of escaping if anything went wrong. What choice did he have, though? If he turned and walked away, he'd blow the whole investigation.

The man flourished his automatic and again said, "Inside—now!"

Joe ducked his head and stepped up into the van, keeping his hands away from his sides. "Hey, man, I'm cool," he protested. "I just want to do some business, you know?"

"Sit down over there," the guy told him, pointing to the rear bench seat. "Now, who sent you? I never seen you before, and you look pretty straight-arrow. Kind of like a cop."

Joe thought fast. "There's a guy I play basketball with. He told me about you."

"Yeah? What's his name?" the gun dealer demanded tensely.

"His street name's Jive," Joe replied, trying to sound relaxed. "I don't know any other name. All the guys call him Jive, that's all."

The man looked puzzled, but Joe was relieved to see that he let the muzzle of the gun dip until it was pointing more at the floor. Joe decided to follow up his advantage. "Hey, that's a nine-millimeter you got there, isn't it?" he said.

The blond guy nodded. "That's right. A fifteen-round clip and enough muzzle velocity to stop a horse. I can get you one tomorrow. Anything we don't have in stock will take a week to ten days. Prices start at two hundred, for a .38 service revolver, and our terms are cash, in used small bills. Any questions?"

Joe scratched his head, then cleared his throat. "Uh—no, sir," he said in a small voice. "I—well, I've got almost two hundred dollars. I could have the rest by next week."

A look of disgust crossed the man's face. "Get out of here," he said, waving the gun. "Come back when you're ready to stop wasting my time."

Joe scrambled out and walked away, his shoulders slumped. He could sense the gun dealer's eyes on him. And he could feel the exact spot between his shoulder blades that would become a bull's-eye if the guy decided to open fire.

Joe went a full block and waited on the corner. A couple of minutes passed, then Frank drove up from the other direction. Joe got in quickly, and Frank put the van in motion.

"Did you run into trouble?" Frank asked.

"If somebody waves a Glock automatic in your face, does that count as trouble?" Joe asked. "No, I came on kinda broke and kinda dumb, and I think he bought it. I hope so. It sounds like he and his friends have enough firepower to outfit a platoon of Rangers."

"So he *is* a gunrunner. How many guns did you actually see?" Frank asked.

"Just the one," Joe replied. "Yeah, I know—he probably keeps the rest stashed somewhere safe. If we tried to get him busted on the basis of the evidence we have now, he wouldn't even get a slap on the wrist."

"No, *we* would, for wasting police time," Frank said. "Still, I vote we keep on this. The kids at HTH have things tough enough as it is, without some slimeball peddling weapons to them like they're water pistols."

As Frank and Joe turned on to their block, they saw their father's car starting up the driveway. Frank gave a faint beep of the horn. Fenton waved, then waited for them next to the garage.

"Hi, Dad," Joe called. "Good trip?"

"It was okay," he replied. "New York isn't my idea of a vacation spot in hot weather. Luckily, I was in air-conditioned offices most of the time. How about the two of you? Are you enjoying your vacation so far?"

"That's a long story," Frank said. "Maybe we should go inside."

"Let's see, where should we start?" Frank said once they were seated in Fenton's office. "With the bank holdup, or the gunrunner?"

"Or nearly getting arrested," Joe added.

Fenton acted alarmed. "Maybe you should start at the beginning," he suggested.

Frank nodded. "Okay. Yesterday around lunchtime, Joe and Callie and I decided to catch a flick at the mall...."

He and Joe took turns recounting the events of the past two days. When they finished, their dad leaned back, gazed up at the ceiling, and thoughtfully tapped his pen against his front teeth.

When he sat up, he said, "I can't say I'm surprised about the gun smuggling. New York has very tough regulations about gun sales, but as long as other states are looser, that just makes gunrunning more profitable. Did you get the license number of the van?"

"Sure," Frank told him. "But it's bound to be a phony."

Fenton swiveled his chair to face the computer. "Let's find out," he said, and entered a series of commands. Joe gave him the license number, and he entered that as well. A moment later he let out a chuckle.

"What is it?" Joe demanded.

"The number belongs to a white Wanderer van, registered in Richmond, Virginia," Fenton told them. "And the name of the owner is Robert E. Lee."

Frank said, "A phony name, Dad?"

Fenton shook his head. "Not necessarily. Lee is a fairly common last name. And in the South, if your last name is Lee, you might be tempted to name your son after the Confederate general."

Frank copied the address and phone number off the screen, then dialed. The man who answered was obviously used to receiving crank calls because of his name. Frank finally convinced him that this one was for real. When he hung up, he said, "Mr. Lee has a white van. It's parked in front of his house right now.

"Last week he went out and found the plates missing. He had to get a new set. He wasn't thrilled."

"So the crooks went looking for the same model and color van as theirs and stole the plates and registration?" Joe said. "Cute. That way, if they're stopped and a cop radios in the number, the motor vehicle records won't give them away."

"That'll weigh against them when they're caught," Fenton said. "But I agree, you need more evidence to take to the authorities."

"We'll be there tomorrow," Frank said. "And this time we'll have our camcorder. What about the bank robberies, Dad? Can you help us?"

"I wish I could, but I can't," Fenton replied. "I have an important meeting in Washington tomorrow morning. If I'm done, I'll fly back in the evening. If not, I'll have to come back Friday. It's a good thing your mom is off in Boston this week. She hates it when I'm away so much."

The next morning Frank and Joe slept late. They weren't due at HTH until that afternoon. They found a note from their father on the breakfast table. " 'Check out bank holdup 6/14 in Seafair'," Joe read out loud. "Seafair sounds familiar."

"Seafair?" Frank repeated. "It's a tiny town about twenty miles from here. I wonder if Con Riley knows about this."

"We could drop by and tell him this morning," Joe suggested. "Maybe he'll be so grateful, he'll let us see those surveillance videos."

"Yeah, sure," Frank replied. "What's the weather going to be?" He tuned the radio on the counter to an all-news station.

"This just in," the announcer said. "Four armed bandits held up the Beehive Savings Bank in the Smithville Mall when it opened this morning. No word yet on how much they stole. Our roving reporter is on her way to the scene."

Frank and Joe stared at each other. Then Frank grabbed the phone and dialed Con Riley.

"I should have known it was you," Riley said when he heard Frank's voice. "You boys have a nose for bad news."

"Was it the same gang?" Frank asked.

"That, or copycats," the police officer replied. "They wore business suits and ski masks, and they fired a few rounds into the ceiling, just to convince people they were serious."

"Can we come by in a little while?" Frank asked. "We may have a lead for you."

Riley said, "I'll be here for half an hour."

At police headquarters Frank and Joe found Con Riley at his desk, scanning a report. When they told him about a possible link between the bank holdup at the mall and the earlier one in Seafair, Riley said, "Thanks. We just connected that robbery to the others, and we're checking it out right now."

His expression became thoughtful. Picking up an unlabeled videocassette, he said, "Now, why would a spare copy of the holdup tape be on my desk? It's terrible the way things get misplaced around here. Excuse me for just a minute. I have to speak to someone down the hall."

He stepped away from his desk. Joe checked the surrounding area. No one around. Then he reached for the cassette and tucked it into his jeans waistband under his T-shirt. Riley strode back to his desk a couple of minutes later and said, "I take it you two guarded my evidence carefully in my absence."

"Of course, Officer Riley," Joe said, pulling out his T-shirt to make sure the bulge the videocassette made in front wasn't obvious.

"We'd better go now," Frank said, breaking in. "We know how busy you are. Thanks for your time, Officer Riley."

"Anytime," Con replied with the hint of a twinkle in his eye.

Outside, Joe asked Frank, "Do you think Con Riley knows I borrowed the tape?"

Frank chuckled. "Know? Not officially. He set it up so that he wouldn't *have* to know.

And besides, that copy of the tape probably doesn't even exist—officially."

"Right," Joe said. "Now, if Vanessa's home, she's got the equipment and know-how to help us analyze this tape.'

Joe called from the cellular phone in the van. When Vanessa heard his voice, she said, "I'm glad you called—I just tried your house. I don't have to work this morning and was hoping you could give me a ride. Is that possible?"

"Sure," Joe replied. "And maybe you could give us a little help. We have a videotape that we need to check out on some really good video equipment."

"Sure, come right over," Vanessa said.

Vanessa lived with her mother, Andrea, in a big old farmhouse outside of town. When Joe and Frank arrived at the back door, Andrea greeted them.

"Hi, guys," she said. "Vanessa will be right down."

A couple of minutes later, Vanessa appeared, wearing white jeans and a navy T-shirt. "Ready to get to work?" she asked.

She led them around the back of the house to the barn that housed Andrea's animation studio. The barn had burned down not long after Vanessa and her mom moved to Bayport, but it was now rebuilt and filled with high-tech hardware.

Vanessa led the way into the studio, and Joe handed her the tape. She put it in a VCR, then directed the signal to a projection TV. The picture, in grainy black and white, showed the interior of the bank branch. The high angle of the shot made the customers appear short and squat.

They watched as the four bandits entered at the lower left of the screen. Their ski masks were almost comical with their business suits, but there was nothing funny about their weapons. Vanessa and the Hardys viewed the entire holdup, then rewound the tape and watched it again.

"Can we get a closer look at the crooks?" Frank asked.

Vanessa tugged at her earlobe. "Yes and no," she said. "We're limited by the lousy quality of the original tape. But maybe if I run the signal to the computer and capture it digitally, I can do a few tricks."

"So what are we waiting for?" Joe demanded.

The three went through the tape again, using the Freeze Frame button each time something interested them. Then they downloaded the images to one of the computer's hard disks.

"What I'm going to do now," Vanessa explained, "is enhance the images electronically." She brought up the first of the captured images on to the monitor. Joe and Frank watched over her shoulder.

"Can we zoom in on the guy in the middle?" Frank asked.

"Sure." Vanessa used the mouse to draw a small rectangle around the central figure, then dragged down a menu and clicked on 10X. The robber's picture filled the screen—or rather, the dots that made it up filled the screen.

"That's not as clear as it was before," Joe complained.

"Enhancement time," Vanessa said. "Cross your fingers." She called up a different menu and quickly made a series of choices, then moved the cursor to OK? and clicked.

"Wow!" Frank exclaimed. "The whole picture just came into focus!"

Vanessa used the same enhancement procedure on the other frames they had selected before sending them all to the laser printer. Within minutes they had the images spread out on a worktable and began studying them.

"How weird," Frank remarked. "They're all wearing high-tops with their suits."

"So they can run faster," Joe suggested with a grin.

Frank picked up one of the prints and looked at it more closely, then compared it with two others. "Wait a minute," he said, pointing to one of the bandits. "That guy's high-tops are laced to look like the rungs on a ladder."

"So?" Vanessa said after a glance. "A lot of people are doing that this summer. Haven't you noticed? It's a fad."

"A fad *among teenagers,*" Frank pointed out.

Joe's eyes widened. "Frank!" he said. "You mean these bank robberies are being pulled off by kids?"

Chapter

9

"ARE YOU GUYS SERIOUS?" Vanessa demanded. "Do you really expect me to believe that there's a gang of teenage bank robbers out there somewhere?"

"Why not?" Frank replied. He tapped his forefinger on the photo they'd been studying. "I'd be surprised if any grown-ups would bother to lace their shoes like this."

Vanessa shook her head. "Look, I know kids commit crimes," she said. "I watch TV and read the papers. But kids usually steal cars, get into gang fights, stick up gas stations, stuff like that. Robbing banks just seems so—I don't know, so *adult.*"

Joe pointed to one of the pictures. "What

do you want to bet that's why they're wearing suits and ties?" he demanded. "To hide their real ages."

"Hold on," Frank said. "Just because we think one of the gang is a teen doesn't mean they *all* are. Let's check out the other pictures."

They carefully studied the images of the other bandits. "No question," Joe finally said. "Three of the four crooks are using that ladder lacing. Either they're kids or they're going to a lot of trouble to make people *think* they're kids."

Vanessa, still unconvinced, studied the prints on the table. "What about the guns?" she asked. "Aren't those high-powered weapons? Where would a teen gang get weapons like that?"

"Right here in Bayport," Frank told her. He went on to explain about the gun-smuggling operation he and Joe had stumbled across.

"As a matter of fact," Joe added, "we found out about it because I overheard a couple of HTH members talking in the locker room."

"A bigger question is how they got hold of the information they obviously have," Frank said. "Bayport High doesn't give a course in silent alarms, rigged bundles of cash, and armored car delivery schedules."

Vanessa's jaw dropped. "Frank!" she said. "That's part of the HTH program!"

"What is? Bank robbery?" Frank demanded.

Vanessa stamped her foot and said, "No, I'm serious! Pat told you how important job training and internships are to the kids in HTH. Well, he managed to get some area banks to agree to take our members as part-time trainees this summer."

Joe stared at her. "Some of the Hands to Help kids are working in banks?" he demanded.

"Well, not yet," Vanessa told him. "The program's just getting under way. So far, only one guy's tried it, and he got bored and left after a couple of weeks. You've met Gil."

"Gil!" Joe exclaimed. "I knew it! I bet he's the ringleader."

"Let's not jump to conclusions, Joe," Frank said. "We're only guessing that some of the bank robbers are teenagers because of the way they lace their high-tops. We do know that some kids at HTH know about buying illegal guns because you heard two of them talking about it."

"We also know that Gil worked in a bank," Joe pointed out. "And we know that he was very, *very* interested that we're detectives. Doesn't any of that add up?"

Frank shuffled through the pictures as he thought about what Joe had said. They had gotten off on the wrong foot with Gil, long before he could have known they were detectives. Gil had a lot of influence with the other kids in HTH. Maybe he saw Joe and Frank as rivals, and that was why he was hostile to them. Maybe the threat he'd overheard Gil making to Vinnie was over some other dispute. Maybe it wasn't. In any case, Frank reminded himself, protecting your territory and being an armed robber were very different.

"I think we'd better do a lot more nosing around at Hands to Help before we start making accusations," Frank suggested. "Maybe some of the kids have heard something that could give us a lead to this gang."

There was a buzz from the console. Vanessa flicked a switch. Her mother's voice said, "Vanessa? There's a call for you."

"Thanks, Mom." Vanessa picked up the telephone. "Hello? Oh, hi, Chet. Welcome back. How's it going?"

Frank looked at Joe. Chet Morton, one of their best friends, had been out of town for a few days.

"No, they're right here," Vanessa said. "Wait, I'll put Frank on."

Frank took the handset from her and said, "Hi, Chet. Good to have you back."

"Hey, it's not like I've been gone for months!" Chet said a bit indignantly. "I talked to Callie last night, and she told me all about that bank robbery at the mall. I bet you and Joe are on the case."

"As a matter of fact, we are," Frank said.

"So why haven't I heard from you?" Chet continued. "Can't use my help?"

Frank rolled his eyes. "Chet, we didn't even know you were back in town," he replied. "But now that we do, why don't we meet at Mr. Pizza at noon and work out a plan of attack?"

"You got it," Chet said, with enthusiasm. "I'll call Phil and Biff and see if they can be there, too. Catch you later."

When Frank, Joe, and Vanessa got to Mr. Pizza, they found Chet already there. He was standing at the counter, talking to Tony Prito, another friend who often helped the Hardys on their cases when he wasn't working at the pizzeria.

"I already ordered a large pie with sausage and mushrooms," Chet announced.

"Why did you do that? You know I don't like sausage," Vanessa said.

Chet grinned. "Don't sweat it. That one's for me. What do you guys want?"

"A wheelbarrow?" Joe suggested. "We'll need it to carry you out of here if you eat a whole pizza."

"Tell you what," Frank added. "As a special favor, we'll help you eat it."

"Not me," Vanessa said quickly. "Tony, could I get a plain slice with extra cheese?"

"Coming right up," Tony replied.

"Anyone else joining us?" Frank asked.

Chet shook his head. "Biff and his family are away," he reported. "And Phil just got a summer job with a computer company."

Tony brought their pizza, then had to go off to serve a customer.

As they ate, Frank and Joe filled Chet in on what they knew—or suspected, so far. Chet's eyes grew wider and wider.

"A gang of teen bank robbers with automatic weapons?" he exclaimed. "We'd better nail them before somebody gets killed. What's the plan?"

"We're going to try to find out what the kids at Hands to Help know first," Joe told him.

"And we're also going to keep an eye on the guys selling illegal guns," Frank added.

"What about me?" Chet asked. "What can I do to help out?"

"Well . . ." Frank cleared away the paper plates and unfolded the map that he had

81

brought in from the van. "Here, take a look. This is Seafair, over here, and here's Smithville, where they hit today. The holdup last week was in Orchard Bay. And here's Bayport, of course. Anybody see a pattern? Something that might tell us something about the gang, or help us guess where they might hit next?"

The others studied the map. "All the towns are on or near major highways," Joe said slowly.

"Makes the getaways easier," Chet suggested.

"Maybe," Vanessa said. "But it could be a coincidence. I wonder if the banks have anything else in common."

"So do I," Frank said. "And the best way to find out is to go have a look at each of them. Chet? How about it? It means a lot of driving."

"I'll get right on it," Chet said, reaching for the last slice of pizza. "As soon as I've finished lunch, that is."

Vanessa glanced at her watch. "Joe, Frank— we've got to go. We don't want to set a bad example by being late. By the way, would you like to drop by my workshop this afternoon? Some of the kids are going to show off the videos they've worked on. It should be pretty neat."

"I'll try," Frank promised. "I don't really know my schedule."

"I don't know mine either," Joe said, "but I'm sure I can do it."

Chet promised to call the Hardys at home that evening with whatever he'd learned. Then he set off.

The trip across town to HTH went quickly. Joe let Frank and Vanessa off near the building entrance, then parked the van. As he was walking back, Pat called to him from the midst of a bunch of kids on the basketball court.

"Joe? Would you mind going by the supply room and bringing out the basketball equipment bag?" he said. "You can't miss it. It's just down the hall."

Pat reached in the pocket of his warm-up suit and pulled out a ring of keys. "Here, catch," he said, tossing them underhand. "It's the one with the yellow plastic ring around it."

Joe scooped the bunch of keys out of midair and went into the building. After taking a wrong turn, he needed a couple extra minutes to find the supply closet. The door wasn't quite closed. Frowning, he pushed it open. The supply room was totally dark. He groped along the doorjamb, found the light switch, and flipped it up. Nothing happened.

Joe's frown deepened. Warily, he stepped inside the room. Something—a faint displacement of air, a darker shape within the shadows—alerted him. He jumped to his left. The open doorway let in just enough light for him to see the baseball bat that was sweeping around directly toward his head.

Chapter

10

JOE DIVED FORWARD, and the baseball bat slammed into the wall. Chips of plaster showered down. Joe had extended his arms to cushion his fall, and the moment he hit the floor, he swung his legs around in a sweeping motion, just at ankle height. His right shin connected with something solid, and he had the satisfaction of hearing a grunt of pain. He made a grab in that direction. His hand closed on a leg, but an instant later it was jerked out of his grasp.

Joe curled up into a ball and threw himself in the direction of the shadowy figure. A baseball bat was a distance weapon. The closer he got to his attacker, the less advantage his attacker would have.

The bat banged down and into one of the metal shelves that ringed the supply room. Then it clattered to the floor. Joe gathered his feet under him and sprang up. Clasping his two hands together, he swung them as if he were the one with a baseball bat. He was hoping to finish the battle by connecting with his opponent's chin, but his aim was too low. He struck the bunched muscles of the shoulder.

An instant later the point of an elbow caught Joe in the solar plexus. He gasped and doubled over. In the few moments it took him to regain his breath, Joe heard his attacker run out the door and slam it behind him. Joe was left in total darkness.

Muttering to himself, Joe groped his way up the door, found the knob, and jerked it open. He already knew what he would see—an empty corridor. His assailant was long gone. And all Joe knew about him was that he stood about six feet—Joe's height—and was probably going to have a bruised, sore shoulder. Some help.

After he pushed the door open all the way, Joe picked up the equipment bag and locked the supply room. He asked himself some questions about the attack. Had he just happened to stumble across a burglary, or was the guy waiting for him? The answer to that one seemed pretty obvious. But if he *was* after Joe, how had he known to wait in the supply room?

Joe recalled that a lot of kids had heard Pat ask him to go for the equipment bag. And he had taken a while to get there. Time enough for someone to get there ahead of him, hide inside, and wait with a baseball bat. The next question was, of the kids who had been outside with Pat, which one had found some excuse to go inside?

At the entrance, Joe met Pat coming in.

"What took you so long, Joe?" the program director demanded.

"I got lost," Joe told him. "Sorry. Did anybody leave or is everybody still out there waiting for me to coach?"

Pat grinned. "If not, I'm sure they'll be right back. On a warm day like this, you can't tell people not to run off to the water fountain, can you? Do you think you can find your way out to the court?"

Joe made a face. "I just might manage," he said.

Frank was the first to arrive for the group session. Someone had arranged folding chairs in a big circle. Frank hesitated in the doorway, then went over and sat down in one of just three chairs that were outside the circle. Even though it was listed on his schedule, he was here to observe the discussion group, not take part in it. If it turned out that he had something to contribute, he could speak from where he was.

Jack Nevins, the electronics executive, was the next to show up. He came over to say hello and shake Frank's hand. "First time for you?" he asked. "I think you'll get a lot out of it. I know I do. These kids are sharp, and they don't have much patience for nonsense."

As the other participants came trickling in, Nevins took a seat across the room from Frank. Once the chairs were filled, he said, "Okay, who's got something on his or her mind? Sabina?"

A shy-looking girl in jeans and a Harvard T-shirt said, "I got to thinking after last time about how everybody is saying it's so important to be good at what you do. But what if you're not? I mean, I like to draw, okay? But I'm not that good at it, I just like it. Are they saying I should give it up because I'm not good?"

There was a babble of voices. Nevins held up his hands. "Hector? What do you think?"

"This is stupid," Hector said. "If Sabina wants to draw, nobody's stopping her. But if she's not good at it, she's not going to make a dime. So how's she going to pay the rent?"

Ricky was halfway around the circle from

Frank. He practically bounced out of his chair, he was so eager to speak. "If she really likes what she's doing, won't that show?" he demanded. "I bet she could sell her drawings for a load of money. Maybe five or ten bucks apiece, even."

Nevins cut in. "Sabina? Is something bothering you?"

"Yeah, I guess so," Sabina responded. "What if Joella turns out to be really super at—I don't know—selling life insurance, and she makes pots and pots of money doing it. But what she really wants to do is write songs and sing them. What good is all that money to her?"

Hector said, "Simple. She can use it to hire a backup band and put out her own disk. Hey, she could probably buy her way onto MTV if she's rich enough. But if she's poor, forget it!"

The discussion continued, but it seemed to Frank that it was losing focus. Finally Nevins said, "What I'm hearing is a lot of confusion about whether you should do something that's personally fulfilling or something you make money at. Am I right?"

Most of the kids in the circle agreed.

"Well, here's something I'd like you to think about, between now and our next meeting," Nevins continued. "What if those two things aren't opposites? What if selling life insurance

89

is fulfilling. That fact will show up in your annual sales figures and your income."

"Yeah, but what about artists or musicians?" a tall boy with a blond ponytail demanded.

"What about them?" Nevins retorted. "There are some artists and musicians who make more money than heads of America's largest corporations. Why? Because they've got what it takes. And you can't argue with success."

There was a silence as the kids in the group absorbed this. Frank wondered if Nevins really meant to say that financial success was the proof of talent. Wasn't it true that many great artists and composers had been financial failures all their lives? And didn't luck, or being born to the right parents, sometimes decide whether a person was successful or not? If making a lot of money automatically meant you were talented, then a successful bank robber must be a genius!

Frank wished he could jump in and make some of these points, but he didn't feel it was the appropriate time. After a few closing remarks from some of the kids, Nevins glanced at his watch. "Okay, that about wraps it up," he said. "We can spend some more time on these issues at the next meeting, if you like."

After leaving the meeting, Frank went by the locker room to pick up Joe, who was just changing out of his basketball clothes. They hurried straight to the classroom where Vanessa's video workshop was getting under way. Joe knocked as Vanessa was beginning to address the class. She said, "I know how much we're all looking forward to sharing our works in progress. To make it easier, I've patched in three of the monitors." She motioned to Frank and Joe and said, "Come on in, guys." Then she addressed the class again. "Did everyone meet Joe and Frank Hardy? They're new counselors here, and I asked them to come by to see what we've been doing."

Joe glanced around the room. Most of the faces were familiar, but other than Vanessa and Frank, the only person he knew by name was Ricky.

"Ricky?" Vanessa said. "Let's start with your tape. Would you like to say something about it before we roll it?"

The boy's face reddened. "Er—not really," he said, glancing around looking for a hiding place.

Vanessa grinned. "Okay, then—here it is." She pressed the Play button on the remote. A cartoon of a sidewalk scene appeared on the screen. A tall, wide character came walking along and bumped into a little guy. The little guy fell down, bounced up, and waved his hand in the big guy's face. This happened three times. Then the big guy shoved the little guy aside and walked on. The little guy pulled out a gun and sprayed bullets at the receding figure of the big guy. The last scene showed the big guy lying on the sidewalk, while the little guy grinned and walked calmly away.

"Hey, okay, Ricky," Vanessa said. "Way to go. You seem really comfortable with the tools, and you know how the elements of a story work together. I'd also like to discuss the message. Any comments?"

"I thought the tape was really cute," a girl in a red tank top said. "I loved the way the little squirt kept bouncing up after he was knocked down. I thought the message was that the big guy doesn't always have to win, that the little guy can win if he gets smart."

"Melanie, do you think it's smart to use a gun to settle an argument?" Vanessa asked.

"Hey," Ricky jumped in, "sometimes the only way for the little guy to come out on top is if he gets some extra muscle."

Vanessa turned to Frank and said, "Frank, do you have any thoughts on that?"

"Well, I wouldn't want to think that the only way for little guys to hold their own with big bullies is to shoot them," Frank replied.

There was a brief silence before Vanessa continued, "Okay, the point is that Ricky's video shows a lot of skill. But I want you to remember, it's important to pay attention to the message. Now, keeping that in mind, why don't we take a look at Sandra's tape?" Vanessa put a new cassette in the VCR. "It's called *Get Back.*"

The screen flickered, then became bright blue. Frank heard a muffled exclamation from one of the watchers.

Three stick figures appeared on the screen. The one wearing a skirt was labeled *Vanessa* in ragged printed letters. The other two were named *Joe* and *Frank*.

"Vanessa! This isn't my tape," a girl with dark hair and a round face insisted.

Vanessa opened her mouth to reply. But at that moment, on the screen, a large object marked 5000 LB fell onto the three stick figures, flattening them.

Frank caught his breath. Across the top of the screen, in bloodred, appeared the words SNOOPERS DIE!

Chapter

11

EVERYBODY GASPED, as the message on the screen sank in. Frank, who glanced over and saw Joe silently mouthing the word "Whoa," was one of the first to recover from the shock. He quickly scanned the other faces in the room. Most looked surprised, even stunned, except Melanie, the girl in the red tank top, who had a slight smile on her face. She looked to Frank as if she might be keeping a big secret—and enjoying it.

"Vanessa, I swear, I had nothing to do with that tape!" Sandra cried.

Vanessa patted her arm. "Of course not, Sandra," she said. "Somebody decided to play a joke, that's all."

Joe said, "May I see the cassette, Vanessa?"

Vanessa pressed the Eject button on the remote, and the tape glided out of the slot. Joe took it from her and closely studied the labels on the front and side of the cassette. Typed on each of them were the words "Get Back by Sandra Peppertone." Joe showed them to Sandra. "Do you recognize these?" he asked.

Sandra's jaw dropped. "Where's my tape?" she demanded near tears. "I worked so hard on it, too."

"This isn't your cassette, then?" Joe asked her.

"Of course not!" she cried. "The clown who did this couldn't even spell my name. It's *Pepitone*, not Peppertone! I wrote all the labels myself, and marked which version was on each cassette."

Vanessa looked over Joe's shoulder and said, "Those labels were done on a dot matrix printer. If you look real close at the curvy letters, you can make out the individual dots."

"Is there a dot matrix printer here at HTH?" Frank asked.

"Sure," Sandra said. "In the word-processing lab. There are a couple of dot matrixes and a laser printer, too."

Joe said, "It wouldn't take more than a minute or two to print this on a label sheet. And there'd be no way to trace who did it."

Vanessa was rummaging around in a nearby cabinet that held mostly videocassettes. "Hey!" she suddenly shouted. "Look, Sandra, here's your tape. Somebody hid it behind these blank tapes. Okay, everybody, now get ready to see the world premiere of the real *Get Back.*"

Joe and Frank stayed behind after the workshop to talk to Vanessa. "How hard would it have been for somebody to make that tape?" Joe asked.

Vanessa tugged at her earlobe and looked up toward the ceiling. "Hmmm—the three figures didn't move at all," she said. "The only animation was the falling dumbbell. With the software we work with here, I could probably duplicate it in five or ten minutes, maybe less."

"Yes, but you're an expert," Frank pointed out. "What about someone who's simply taken your class? Could he or she do it?"

Vanessa laughed. "If they couldn't, I'm not much of an instructor. Hey, you saw Ricky's tape, and Sandra's. Both of them used far more complicated techniques than anything on that other tape."

Joe said, "Then anybody who's taken your

class could have done it? Is there a lot of access to the equipment?"

"The room's open all day," Vanessa said. "It's the only way the kids can have the time to put together anything worthwhile. I had to fight for it, but so far it's worked out."

"Can you tell me anything about that girl, Melanie?" Frank asked, recalling the odd expression on the girl's face when the threatening tape was played.

Vanessa gave him a curious look. "Melanie? I've had some problems with her. She doesn't like to admit that anybody might have anything to teach her. And I've heard she got in a lot of fights at her school."

"Who does she hang with?" asked Joe.

"Gil and his bunch," Vanessa replied with a shrug.

"Somehow I just knew you were going to say that," Joe said. "That guy has had an attitude since we arrived. I haven't even had a chance to tell you what happened this morning."

Joe recounted his visit to the supply room and the fight in the dark against an attacker armed with a baseball bat. "I didn't get a look at him," he said, "but I'm willing to bet his name starts with *G* and has three letters."

"Do you have any proof of that?" Frank asked.

"Well, no," Joe admitted. "But I'm going to

do my best to find some. And when I do, it's 'Watch out, Gil!' ''

The rest of the afternoon seemed to pass quickly. Frank and Joe drove Vanessa home. Then, after a stop by their house to pick up the camcorder and tell their aunt Gertrude they wouldn't be back in time for dinner, they drove across town.

"I'm going to look for a spot to park where we'll have a good angle for taping anybody who goes near the van," Joe said.

"Good thinking," Frank said. "If he shows up at all, that is. For all we know, he only comes to Bayport on Wednesdays."

Joe shot him a dirty look and said, "We just arrived for the big stakeout, and my own brother is already telling me there's a good chance we're wasting our time. Don't forget, Frank, yesterday the guy said he'd deliver whatever I ordered today."

"But you *didn't* order anything," Frank pointed out. "Still, detective work is nine-tenths following leads that don't work out. But if you don't follow every lead, how will you ever find the one-tenth that *do* work out?"

Joe rolled his eyes and said, "All I wanted was a little reassurance. And instead, what do I get? Philosophy!"

Frank laughed and aimed a fist at Joe's biceps.

"Please!" Joe protested. "Not while I'm driving."

Joe went south, then turned right and slowed down. "I'll have to park at a hydrant," he announced. "Do you have a problem with that?"

"Not if the cops or the fire department don't," Frank replied. As Joe pulled into the illegal parking space, Frank slipped in between the two seats and sat on the floor next to the big window, which was tinted black. The camcorder was at hand. He checked the battery charge and the cassette, then tried to relax.

"The white van's there," Joe reported.

Frank glanced out the window, then tried looking through the viewfinder of the camcorder. He had a clear shot at the curbside door of the gun smuggler's van. "Right here is fine," he called.

Joe set the parking brake and turned off the engine, then slipped back to join Frank.

"No action so far," Joe said, peering through the one-way window. "I hope we're not wasting our time."

"We're not," Frank said, his voice rising. "Look who's here."

A car had pulled up a few spaces behind the

white van. The driver's door opened—and Gil stepped out.

"I *knew* it," Joe exclaimed. "I never liked that guy from the minute I saw him."

Frank grabbed his arm and squeezed it. There was someone else in the car. The door on the passenger side opened—and out climbed Pat McMillan.

Chapter

12

"TURN ON THE CAMCORDER," Frank blurted. "Quick—we've got to get this on tape!"

Joe pressed the Record button and hit the rocker switch to zoom in on Gil and Pat. The two approached the van and spoke to whoever was within. Then they ducked their heads and stepped inside. The sliding door closed.

Joe switched the camcorder to Pause and looked over at Frank. "Pat McMillan?" he said in a mixture of pain and disbelief. "I thought he was such a great guy."

"So did I," Frank said soberly. "But let's face it. If you were planning to put together a gang, what better way to recruit members than by starting a program for teens who've had run-ins with the law? While you were pretending to help them to go straight, you'd really be encouraging them to go on breaking the law."

"And if they got caught," Joe added, "you'd just say, 'Tut, tut,' and throw up your hands. It's perfect. It's . . . fiendish."

"Watch it, they're coming out of the van," Frank said.

Joe followed Pat and Gil with the camcorder, as they left the gun seller's van and walked back to their car. He made a point of zooming in, first on their faces, then on the license plate of their car as they drove off.

"Hey, the van's leaving, too," Frank exclaimed. "Quick, let's follow."

Joe quickly handed the camcorder to his brother and jumped into the driver's seat. Frank stowed the camcorder in its case, then climbed into the passenger seat and fastened his seat belt.

The white van pulled out from the curb and drove north. Joe dropped back a little. He figured that anyone dealing in illegal guns might be easily spooked, so he didn't want to follow too closely.

The chase led across Bayport to a motel not far from the interstate interchange. Joe pulled into the parking lot and got out to follow the driver to his room. A couple of minutes later, he returned and said, "Room

Two twenty-eight. Frank, the pool looks very inviting. Do you think we have enough time for a swim?"

"Next visit," Frank replied. "And we'll have to remember to bring our suits. Come on, let's see if a little teamwork can help us put a name to Mister Two twenty-eight."

They walked over to the motel office. Frank asked the manager how to get to a restaurant called Le Manoir on the other side of town. The manager took him over to a big map of the Bayport area and began to explain. Frank listened, nodding from time to time.

Meanwhile, Joe was quickly scanning the motel's register. Once he had what he was after, he rejoined Frank and the manager. "All set?" he asked, clapping Frank on the shoulder.

"Sure," Frank said, then added to the manager, "Okay, thanks a bunch."

Back in the van, Frank said, "Well? Who is he?"

"Would you believe R. E. Lee, of Richmond, Virginia?" Joe replied, disgusted.

"Surprised?" Frank said. "Don't forget, ever since he stole Mr. Lee's plates and registration, he's had a very convenient alias."

Frank reached for the cellular phone, then shrugged and put it back in its mount without dialing. "I was going to call Con, but on second thought I don't think we have enough to take

103

to the authorities yet," he said reluctantly. "Let's go home."

"Great idea," Joe said. "I bet Aunt Gertrude left something in the fridge for us."

They were sitting at the kitchen table, finishing the last of a reheated tuna casserole, when they heard a car pull into the garage. A few moments later Fenton Hardy came in the back door.

"Hello, boys. Did you save me any dinner?" he asked, then quickly added, "Just joking. I had something on the plane. I'm not quite sure what it was, but the flight attendant swore it was dinner."

"Can I fix you a sandwich, Dad?" Frank asked. "There are some cold cuts."

Fenton shook his head. "No, thanks."

"How was Washington?" asked Joe.

"Hazy, hot, and humid," his dad replied. "As usual. But I was lucky. I knew one of the committee staffers, and she juggled the schedule to let me testify early, so I could catch a late shuttle back."

"You didn't mention what you were testifying about," Frank said.

Fenton poured himself a glass of iced tea and sat down. "The committee is looking at ways to track down people who avoid paying child support. I was asked to talk about the ins and outs of finding people who don't want to be found. I explained how it's getting harder and harder to drop out of sight. Unless you construct an entirely new identity—birth certificate, driver's license, Social Security number, phone number, credit cards—you're bound to leave electronic footprints that a competent investigator can trace."

He took a swallow of iced tea, then added, "For example, I just bought a CD-ROM that contains practically every telephone directory in the United States. Say you're looking for a man named Ignatz Kabop. You don't even have to know what part of the country he lives in. Enter his name, press a few keys, and if he has a listed phone anywhere in the fifty states, you'll have his address and number in a few seconds."

"That's pretty amazing," Frank said. "Say—does it work in reverse, too? Can you enter a phone number and find out whose it is?"

"It's supposed to, but I haven't tried it out yet," Fenton admitted. "Why?"

Frank said, "I was just thinking—when you combine that with one of those caller ID units that tells you the number a call is coming from, you've just made anonymous phone calls impossible. That's bad news for crank callers."

"It also rules out calling in an anonymous tip to the police," Joe said.

"There are always pay phones," Fenton said.

"Speaking of tips, did you have a chance to look into that bank holdup in Seafair?"

"Not yet," Frank replied. "We've had a pretty full day. And it's just possible that we got a big break in the case." He told his father about spotting Pat and Gil at the van. "Not only that, Pat placed Gil in a trainee's job at a bank a few weeks ago," he added.

"So now we know where the inside information could have come from," Joe said. "All we really need is some direct evidence."

"You're making progress," Fenton said. "Have you checked which bank this fellow Gil works for, and when he started?"

Frank caught Joe's eye, then said, "Not yet. We just found out about his job."

"Dad, is there anything special about the Seafair bank robbery?" Joe asked.

"It struck me that the way it was carried out sounded like the two holdups you told me about," Fenton said. "So did the description of the perpetrators."

"There was another robbery this morning," Frank told him. "In Smithville."

Fenton raised one eyebrow. "Really? They're picking up the pace, aren't they? I wonder if it's because they're confident or desperate." He stood up and stretched. "Well, gentlemen, I'd better go check the mail and listen to my messages. See you in the morning."

A few minutes later Chet called. Frank put him on the speakerphone.

"I checked out those banks," Chet said. He sounded tired. "Four different bank companies in four different towns. One inside a mall, one in a smaller shopping center, one on a downtown street, and one sitting by itself on a corner. I wonder if the robbers deliberately chose them to be as different as possible."

"Did you notice any similarities?" Joe asked.

"Oh, sure," Chet replied. "They all have cash machines. Not to mention doors, windows, air-conditioning, lots of money in small bills . . ."

"We get the idea," Frank told him. "Well, thanks anyway."

Chet gave a snort. "No problem. Oh, and I took instant photos of all of the banks. I'll drop them by your house tomorrow."

He hung up. Joe looked at Frank and said, "That sounds like a dead end."

"But we've got enough other leads to follow," Frank said. "Let's get some rest and see what we can come up with tomorrow."

The next morning the Hardys were a couple of blocks away from Hands to Help when Joe noticed a railroad trestle across the street ahead. Somebody was standing on it, looking down at the traffic. Didn't the guy realize how dangerous that could be if a train came along?

Maybe he did. As the van drew closer, the figure on the overpass vanished. But there was still something up there, the size and shape of a small carton. Joe was asking himself what it might be, when he saw it topple over the edge.

Chapter

13

As the object fell directly toward their windshield, Joe shouted, "Hold on, Frank!" He cranked the wheel all the way to the right and gave one quick, hard jab at the brake pedal. The van swerved wildly, tires screaming. Its rear wheels lost traction and the back end began to slide. For one awful moment Joe was sure they were going to turn over. Instead, the van slid into the curb, just as the heavy carton crashed to the pavement a couple of feet away.

A passing truck blared its horn as they screeched to a stop.

"What happened?" Frank asked.

Joe said, "Somebody tried to drop something on us. A cinder block in a carton, from the looks of what's left of it. Let's see if we can catch him."

He jumped out of the van and scrambled up the side of the railway embankment. Frank was just a few steps behind. They reached the top in time to catch a glimpse of a figure disappearing into the underbrush about a hundred yards up the track.

Joe broke into a run, but the loose gravel and awkwardly spaced ties made it impossible to go very fast. By the time he reached the spot where he had glimpsed the figure, all he could see was the back of the former school that housed Hands to Help. He took a deep breath, kicked at the gravel, and turned back.

Frank was out on the trestle examining the railing. Joe joined him. "Find anything?" he asked.

"Some fresh scratches," Frank replied. "That cement block didn't fall all by itself."

"I knew that," Joe told him. "I saw someone up here. If I hadn't, the cement block would have come right through our windshield. Somebody has a very sick sense of humor."

"Somebody's starting to get desperate," Frank said. "This gang must think we're closing in. It's a good thing they don't realize how little we know for sure. When crooks panic, they start making mistakes that give them away."

As they started down the embankment to the van, Joe said, "As long as one of their dumb mistakes doesn't give *us* away—to the undertaker!"

On his way to his martial arts workshop, Frank ran into Lisa in the corridor.

"Oh, hi," she said with a smile. "I was just thinking about you. How do you like HTH so far?"

"Our first couple of days have been very eventful," Frank said wryly.

"Oh, really?" Lisa responded, puzzled. "Well, I suppose that's better than being bored. Hey, somebody told me that you and your brother are detectives. Is that true?"

"More or less," Frank said.

"That's fascinating," she continued. "I love a good mystery. Are you working on anything now?"

"Sort of," Frank said cautiously. He knew it was a bad idea to talk about ongoing investigations.

Lisa's eyes widened with interest. "Tell me all about it! I would be so thrilled to be able to follow along."

"Usually we just stumble along without knowing how it's going to come out until the end," said Frank, noting how friendly Lisa was acting.

"Sure, that's the way it is in mystery stories," Lisa said with a little laugh. "But I'm one of those awful people who can't resist skipping ahead to the last chapter to find out 'who done it.' Maybe you could clue me in on your investigation. I won't tell anybody. Please?"

"I can't really say anything now," Frank told her. "But maybe in a few days . . ."

The workshop began with a series of warm-up exercises from an ancient Chinese discipline called Chi Qong. When it ended, Lisa, who was all business again, said, "Frank, would you work with Hector on his blocks?"

"Sure," Frank replied. Hector was a powerful, broad-shouldered guy of medium height who had been studying with Lisa the longest. He had very short dark hair and a wary expression in his brown eyes. Frank led him to a corner of the room and asked, "Let's say I throw a punch at your chest? How do you counter it?"

"I block it," Hector replied. His tone indicated that he thought it was a dumb question.

Frank stayed cool. "Right," he said. "But there are lots of possible blocks. Your job is first, to know them, and second, to know which one to use. Here, I'll show you what I mean. In slow motion, take a swing at me."

Hector's idea of slow motion was a little faster than Frank's, but that wasn't a problem. In sequence, Frank demonstrated an outside block, an inside block, a palm-heel block, and a hand-sword block. "You're familiar with all of these?" he asked.

"Yeah, sure," Hector replied. "This is kid stuff."

"Oh? Well then, let's get to work." Frank cocked his right fist at shoulder height and counted "one-two-three" as he aimed it at Hector's chest. Hector used an inside block against it, hitting Frank's wrist with the side of his left forearm. He used more force than necessary, but Frank blunted the blow by letting his arm drift outward.

"Again," Frank said. Hector again used an inside block, this time at full speed and force.

"This is practice, not a meet," Frank said as he evaded Hector's block and tapped him lightly on the chest. "I want to see you use some of the other blocks—and in slow motion. The point of practice is to train your muscles and nerves. That way, when the time comes, they'll do what they need to do automatically."

Hector's face was red, and the muscles of his jaw were tense. This time, as Frank's fist moved across the space between them, he let loose with a wicked hand-sword thrust. If the outer edge of his hand had connected, it would certainly have broken Frank's wrist.

Frank was expecting something of the sort, though. He made his fist circle Hector's thrust, then went in over his forearm and tapped him again on the chest, a little harder this time.

Hector's response was to uncork a full-out right at Frank's beltline.

At this point Frank's patience had worn very thin. He deflected the blow with his right hand, brought his left around to lock Hector's elbow, and used his left leg to sweep Hector's right foot out from under him. Hector ended up flat on his back, with Frank gripping and twisting his wrist.

"Ow!" Hector yelled. "Stop it, you're hurting me!"

Frank released his arm and took a step back, staying on guard. "It's important to keep a cool head and not lose your temper in a bout," he said. "Maybe next time you'll remember that lesson."

Lisa hurried over. "Frank, I asked you to help him practice, not to fight him," she said. "You must learn much more patience and discipline before you can teach the martial arts. I think it's best if you leave now. We can talk more about this later."

Frank thought of explaining, but why bother? Lisa was right: he could easily have evaded or blocked Hector's blow without using a throw that humiliated and maybe even hurt the guy. But he had let his determination to teach the guy a lesson get the better of him.

Shaking his head, Frank walked silently toward the door. Lisa and Hector watched him go. When Frank looked back, he thought he saw the hint of a smile on Hector's face.

"De-fense! *De*-fense!" Joe shouted as Gil stole the rebound from one of Joe's teammates and came racing down the court toward him. Joe moved in closer, arms spread wide and high, hoping to wreck Gil's try at a three-pointer.

Gil charged straight at him. Joe backpedaled, but not quite fast enough to avoid the shoulder blow aimed at his throat. Only superb reflexes saved Joe from the impact. As it was, Gil charged into him and seemed surprised when Joe stayed upright.

"Okay, Gil," Joe growled, squaring off with clenched fists. "I've had it with your bad attitude and your dirty play. Next time you intentionally foul me or anybody else, I'm going to make you pay. Is that clear?"

"You better not try it," Gil retorted as the other players gathered around them. "You and your brother come waltzing in here, acting like you own the place. You think you're so great, giving your time to help us poor underprivileged kids. Who asked you?"

Joe took a deep breath, then said evenly, "Pat did, for one. And it's not my fault if I'm a better basketball player than you are. It's not your fault, either—it's a fact of life. You'll get better, if you let yourself learn. But I'm not going to let you play dirty anymore. That's it."

Gil's body tensed up. Joe was sure that he was about to pound him. He almost hoped so. He'd love to have an excuse to deck this guy.

From the sidelines, Pat called, "Joe? Would you come here, please?"

Joe pushed through the circle of onlookers and walked off the court to where Pat was waiting.

"This is starting to get out of hand," Pat began.

"I know," Joe replied. "But Gil is going to have to learn sportsmanship, whether he likes it or not."

"That's not exactly what I mean," Pat said. "I really appreciate the way you agreed to help out, but I'm not sure you have the right attitude for a Hands to Help counselor. It seems there's been nothing but trouble since you arrived. And I'm sorry to say that the same goes for your brother, Frank. Just a little while ago, he lost his cool and almost injured one of the students in Lisa's martial arts class. I'm afraid

I'm going to have to ask the two of you to leave."

Joe stared at the program director with narrowed eyes. Was it possible that he really believed what he was saying? Gil was making trouble before Joe and Frank even walked onto the scene! And Frank losing his cool? Impossible! There was something behind this, that was obvious.

When Joe didn't say anything, Pat added, "I don't want any more trouble."

'Then let's hope you don't get any," Joe retorted, fed up. He turned and went off in search of Frank.

As the Hardys started for home, Frank said, "The whole thing smells of a setup. Pat must have realized that we were dangerously close to uncovering his scheme. He tried to get rid of us by dropping a concrete block through our windshield. And in case that didn't work, he cooked up a plan to chase us away from HTH. Gil and Hector must have been working with him."

"Well, if he thinks that's going to stop our investigation, he's in for a shock," Joe replied. "I wonder why he wanted us to sign on as counselors in the first place."

"He probably figured by having us around, no one would suspect he had anything to hide. We were all just part of his cover!"

Joe glanced in the mirror, and said, "Uh-oh. It looks like that car is on our tail."

Frank checked his mirror. A dark sedan with two grim-faced men in it was pulling up alongside the Hardys' van. Joe sped up, but the sedan kept pace and began to edge over to the right, forcing the Hardys toward the curb.

Suddenly the guy in the passenger seat reached out the window and fastened a flashing red light to the car's roof. Then he flashed a badge and pointed to the side of the road.

"What do you suppose the cops want now?" Joe wondered. He slowed down, moving onto the shoulder.

The unmarked car swerved in ahead of them and stopped. The two jumped out with guns drawn. Frank glanced back and saw a black and white pull up close behind the van. He felt a spurt of indignation. He and Joe were doing their best to help the police, and all they got for it was hassles!

"Whatever it is," he murmured, "they obviously mean business."

"Step outside with your hands up," a loudspeaker blared. "I repeat—"

Joe and Frank did as they were told. They were quickly frisked, then led to the rear of the van.

"Please open the rear door," one of the plainclothes officers said.

"It isn't locked," Frank replied. "See?"

He reached forward, turned the handle, and pulled the door open. His jaw dropped in surprise. A plastic shopping bag was lying on its side, partly hidden by the rear seat. The bag was stuffed with neatly wrapped bundles of cash, which spilled out all over the floor.

Chapter

14

THE TALLER of the two detectives took a card from his shirt pocket and began to read them their rights. "You have the right to remain silent . . ." When he finished, the uniformed officers handcuffed Frank's and Joe's wrists behind their backs and led them over to the police cruiser.

"Look, this is all a big mistake," Joe said as the car pulled away from the curb. "Ask Chief Collig. He knows us. What are we under arrest for, anyway?"

The two officers in the front seat of the cruiser didn't answer.

"We've been at Hands to Help all morning,"

Frank added. "There are dozens of people who saw us and can testify to that."

"Save it for the judge," the officer at the wheel said.

As Frank and Joe were being led inside police headquarters, an officer who was coming out said to one of the arresting officers, "Those two again? I bet they won't get off so easily this time. What did you nab them for?"

Frank looked up and recognized him. It was Sergeant Hernandez, who had burst in on him and Joe at the diner on Tuesday, after the bank holdup at the mall.

"Suspicion of armed robbery," the police officer holding Joe's arm replied. "Anything else you have on them, you should pass on to Sergeant Lundy. He's got this file."

"I'll do that," Hernandez said. "Armed robbery, huh? Real tough guys."

Inside, Frank and Joe were put in separate interrogation rooms. While he waited, Frank tried to think through what had just happened. Obviously someone had planted that money in the back of the van, then tipped off the police. The question was, when, where, why, and who? Joe had taken his gym bag out of the back when they arrived at Hands to Help that morning. There hadn't been a bag of money in there then. That answered not only when but where. Why was obvious, too. It was another attempt to distract the Hardys from investigating the bank holdups. But this time, in their desperation to ward off the investigation, maybe the gang had finally made a fatal slipup—they had used some of the loot from the holdups to try to set up the Hardys, and now that crucial evidence was in police hands.

Frank didn't have to think too long or hard about who. No one but Pat had known that the Hardys would be leaving a lot earlier than planned.

Two detectives entered the room and sat down at the table in the center. One looked up at the video camera mounted on the wall and announced the date and time, then said, "Detectives Lundy and Martoff are questioning"—he glanced at his notebook—"Frank Hardy. Hardy, you've been informed of your rights, is that correct?"

"Yes, sir," Frank replied. "And I'd like to call my father and tell him we're here."

The two police officers exchanged a glance. "All in due time," said the one Frank guessed was Lundy. "Do you waive your right to have an attorney present?"

Should he? He didn't really have anything to hide—just the opposite—but a mistake now could mean very serious trouble. Frank wished he could talk to Joe for just two minutes, but he knew the cops would never allow it.

"No, I don't," he said. "I want an attorney here. But before we get into any of that, we could all save each other a lot of time if you would give my father a call. You may have heard of him. His name is Fenton Hardy. And you might also tell Chief Collig that my brother and I are here. He'll want to know."

The officers exchanged another glance. Then Lundy said, "Keep an eye on him. I'll go check this out."

After their father came down to identify them and talk to the authorities, it still took an hour for the police and the district attorney's office to decide to let Frank and Joe go free. Chief Collig summoned the three Hardys to his office to give them the news and added, only half jokingly, "I hope you're not planning any Caribbean vacations in the next few weeks."

"No, sir," Frank said. "We're going to stay right here and find out who tried to frame us."

Joe said, "We know who—the bank robbers. That money in our van *was* from one of the holdups, wasn't it?"

Chief Collig frowned down at his desk, then said, "No harm in telling you, I guess. Yes, it was. Over ten thousand in new bills, numbered in sequence."

"And I'll bet you'd already circulated a list.

of the serial numbers," Frank said. "In other words, those bills were practically worthless to the robbers and potentially dangerous. At least they would be pretty hard to get rid of. And how did you know to stop us?"

The chief scowled. "An anonymous phone call," he admitted. "The caller described your van, said where you'd be, and told the desk sergeant that some of the bank holdup loot was in the back."

"It was, too. But what about the rest?" Fenton wondered. "Do you have those serial numbers, too?"

Collig shook his head. "Not really. These guys usually managed to grab used, untraceable bills. They seem to know their business. Now, Fenton, if you'll take your boys home, I'll get on with *my* business. . . ."

On the steps of police headquarters, Fenton looked at his watch and said, "I have an appointment. I'll call you at home later."

"Sure, Dad," Joe replied. "Thanks for bailing us out."

"What's a father for?" Fenton said with a smile. "Oh—and this time, check to make sure no one's left any early Christmas presents in your car."

"What a day," Joe said as they drove home. "First we get canned from our volunteer jobs, then we're arrested as bank robbers."

"You forgot the concrete block," Frank pointed out.

"No, I didn't," Joe insisted. "But with everything else, I was counting that as a mere diversion."

Frank grinned. "You talk like you've been watching too much *Masterpiece Theatre*. Seriously, though, how are we going to nail Pat and Gil?"

"We could just give the cops what we've got and let them take it from there," Joe said, sounding discouraged.

"What do we really have?" Frank asked. "Some of the crooks wear high-tops that they lace in an unusual way. Someone hid that loot in the back of our van."

"While it was parked at HTH," Joe said.

"According to us," Frank reminded him. He shook his head in frustration. "I'm sure there's something we're overlooking, Joe. There must be some common link, some reason the crooks chose to hit those particular banks."

Joe slowed down to turn into the Hardys' driveway. As he came to a stop, he said, "Maybe those happen to be the ones Gil managed to get information about."

"What bothers me about that," Frank said as they walked across the yard to the back door, "is how would he, just starting as a trainee, get sensitive information about security arrangements. Arrangements not just in his bank, but others also?"

Joe paused and scratched his head. "Maybe Pat got the information when he was going around setting up the trainee program," he suggested.

"Yeah, right," Frank said. " 'Thanks for agreeing to hire one of our teens, and by the way, what days do you get your shipments of cash, so we'll be sure there's plenty around when we stick up your bank?' "

Joe rolled his eyes and said, "Okay, so it wasn't one of my best ideas. Can you do any better?"

"Yeah, let's each get a nice cold soda, sit in the shade, and wait for inspiration to hit," Frank replied.

"Great," Joe said. "I'll get the sodas. You get the inspiration."

When Joe went out to the yard, Frank was in a lawn chair under the big oak, frowning. Some instant photos were scattered on his lap.

"Chet left these for us," he said. "I've been trying to figure out what they have in common."

Joe shrugged. "We asked Chet that before. He didn't have an answer. Do you?"

"Maybe," Frank said. "One's in a mall, one's in a smaller shopping center, and so on— but all of them are in buildings that look as if they went up in the last few years."

Joe took the photos and thumbed through them. Then he nodded, "Okay, I agree. So what?"

"We wanted a link," Frank said, "and we may have one. Now, how do we check it out?"

"Isn't there a construction trade newspaper for the area?" Joe asked. "I bet it's on one of the computer databases."

Frank stood up. "Let's find out."

It took almost twenty minutes to locate the network files on construction journals. Once there, they set up a search program for the four banks that had been robbed, and downloaded the information to their own computer.

"Yikes," Frank said when the process was completed. "I didn't realize those companies had been expanding so much. We must have a dozen different files to sift through."

"Let's narrow the search down to stories about the branches that were held up," Joe suggested. "We can go back and sift through the others later if necessary."

The trade paper had listings of all new construction. For each building, there was information about architects, contractors, subcontractors, and suppliers. Both Frank and Joe read through the four relevant stories, then reread them.

"Notice anything?" Joe asked, excitement bubbling just under the surface of his words.

"Yep," Frank replied. "The only common

element is the alarm systems subcontractor, SysAlarmics, Inc. The next question is, who's that?"

They returned to the computer and accessed a database called Edgar that listed information on tens of thousands of companies. SysAlarmics was there, with a notation that it was owned by Nevatronics, Inc.

"Nevatronics!" Joe exclaimed. "That's Jack Nevins's company."

"Interesting," Frank replied. "Let's see what else we can find out about it."

He typed in a new set of commands, studied the screen, and added, "From the looks of the most recent data filed with the Securities and Exchange Commission, I'd say that Nevatronics is in pretty serious financial trouble. Maybe serious enough to make its majority stockholder take desperate measures to save it."

Joe finished the thought. "Such as getting cash any way he can—maybe even by robbing banks?"

Chapter

15

FRANK AND JOE used their father's new CD-ROM telephone index to find Jack Nevins's home address. He lived in a small, exclusive community a few miles east of Bayport.

"That's a problem," Joe pointed out. "I know that area. They've got a local guard service that patrols the area. If we try to stake out Nevins's house, they'll spot us and chase us off."

"Hmm—" Frank replied. "I think I have an idea how to pull it off. . . ."

Early the next morning, after a quick breakfast of cereal with fruit, the Hardys set off for Nevins's. Over their jeans and T-shirts, they were wearing white coveralls with Northfield Tree Service embroidered on the backs. Frank had rounded the uniforms up from their friends Biff and Chet, who had worked at the company the previous summer.

It took a while to locate Nevins's house. Many of the narrow, winding lanes in his neighborhood did not have street signs. Even when the Hardys managed to find the right street, very few of the houses were numbered.

"What do you suppose delivery people do?" Joe wondered as he slowed down to look at the name on still another mailbox.

"The same as we're doing, I guess," Frank replied. "The idea is, if you don't already know where you're going, you probably shouldn't be here. Look," he added, his tone changing. "That must be it on the left. Don't slow down, just pull over and park around the next curve."

Joe risked a quick glance as he drove by. The house was big and rambling and sat on top of a small rise. The garage was on the basement level. A red sports car was sitting in the drive. Its license plate read NEVATRON.

"Three guesses whose car that is," Joe said as he pulled onto the shoulder and stopped.

Frank grinned. "I noticed him drive up in it at Hands to Help yesterday."

Frank opened the glove compartment and took out a plastic box. Inside, cushioned by foam padding, was a device not much bigger than a postage stamp, with a tiny, powerful magnet on one side. Frank opened the case, inserted a fresh watch battery, and closed the lid. Then he flipped down a panel on the dashboard, revealing a small LCD screen marked with a grid pattern. He turned on the switch. A dot immediately appeared in the dead center of the grid.

"So far, so good," he murmured, zipping the device in the breast pocket of his coverall. "Here, take this." He reached into the rear seat, grabbed two clipboards with yellow pads on them, and handed one to Joe.

"Okay. Now what?" Joe asked.

"Stand by the side of the road, look at the trees, and take notes," Frank replied. "If a patrol car comes along, give the guys a friendly wave. I'll be back as quick as I can."

Frank got out of the van and walked briskly up the lane toward Nevins's house. As he approached, he tilted his head back, as if looking up at the treetops. He was actually scanning the windows of the house without seeming to. Most of the drapes were drawn, and he saw no sign of anyone. Maybe Nevins slept late on weekends.

Frank strolled up Nevins's driveway, still peering at the trees. Just as he reached the rear end of the red sports car, he dropped his ballpoint pen. When he bent down to pick it up, the bulk of the car hid him from the house. With smooth, deft movements, he took the tracking transmitter from his pocket and slipped it up into the rear fender well. The powerful magnet held it in place.

Frank stood up, made a note on his pad, and walked back to the van. Less than a minute later, he and Joe were on their way.

"Any problems?" Joe said.

"Not so far," Frank replied. "Let's get out of these coveralls, then head for that shopping center on Route Three-oh-four. Anyone leaving here has to drive right by there. We can take turns monitoring the tracker screen, while the other one window-shops."

"Wouldn't it be better if we both stayed with the van?" Joe asked.

Frank shook his head. "I don't think so. We don't want to attract attention. One guy sitting in a parked car is obviously waiting for somebody. But two guys sitting in a parked car are up to something."

The next hour and a half passed very slowly. During one of his turns on watch, Joe stared at the tracker screen for so long that he began to see spots. And during Frank's watches, Joe prowled the shopping center until he was sure he could describe all the store windows from memory. He was flipping through a bin of discount CD's outside the record shop when he heard a horn give two short, one long, and two short beeps. That was their signal. He hurried to the parking lot, just as Frank was pulling out of the slot.

"He's coming this way," Frank said, driving toward the exit. "With luck, we'll be able to make visual contact."

Joe studied the tracker screen. The dot was almost at the center spot that marked the van's location. Joe looked up and scanned the approaching traffic. "Is that him, about six cars back?" he asked.

"Let's chance it," Frank replied. The light at the corner changed, bringing the stream of cars to a halt. Joe pulled out of the parking lot and crossed the four lanes of traffic, then stopped on the shoulder. Moments later the red sports car passed them slowly enough for Joe to recognize Nevins at the wheel. With a tight smile, Frank let two more cars pass, then pulled out onto the road. The chase was on.

Some chase! Joe was thinking, forty-five minutes later. They had followed Nevins to a fruit store, a butcher shop, a bakery, and a delicatessen. At each stop, he went in and came out a few minutes later with a bag that he put in the trunk of the car.

"He's not planning a bank robbery," Joe groused, after Nevins stopped at a convenience store for a bag of charcoal. "He's having a barbecue."

"Patience, patience," Frank replied with a grin. "We could be at this for days before he does anything incriminating—if he ever does."

The red car turned in at a hamburger place. "Now what?" Joe demanded. "Doesn't he have enough food in the trunk?"

Frank didn't reply. A car turning left from the opposing lane of traffic was blocking the way into the fast-food place. Frank waited, then followed the car into the lot. The driver stopped for another car that was backing out of a slot. Frank drummed his fingers on the steering wheel.

Finally the lane was clear. He pulled forward, scanning the lot for the red car. "Joe?" he said, with a touch of urgency in his voice. "Do you see him?"

Joe in turn searched the lot. "I don't think he's here," he announced. He leaned forward to examine the monitor. "Frank! He's moving away, fast!"

Muttering to himself, Frank drove around the burger place to the drive-through exit. That was obviously what Nevins had done, too. Had he spotted Frank and Joe following him? Or had he simply decided to take a few precautions? "Which way?" he demanded.

"Back to the left," Joe replied. "He's a mile or so ahead of us, still well within range."

It seemed like a long time before a break in the traffic allowed Frank to pull onto the road. He kept the van within the speed limit but took advantage of every gap in traffic to move up a few places.

"He turned right and picked up speed," Joe announced. "He must be taking the expressway."

Frank made a face. They could easily miss an off-ramp on the expressway and have to go miles out of their way. Just as their speedometer needle was touching fifty-five, Joe said, "He's slowing down. Oops—there he goes."

Frank looked ahead. Two exits for Route 130 were coming into sight, one northbound and the other southbound. Which one had Nevins taken? "Which way do I go?" Frank asked, slowing down.

"I can't tell yet," Joe told him. "Wait—okay, north. North!"

Too late. The van was already passing the northbound exit. Frank flipped on the turn signal and pulled onto the off-ramp for south. Once on Route 130, he started looking for a place to make a U-turn. The next one didn't come along for a mile and a half. "Do you still have him?" Frank demanded.

"No problem," Joe replied. "And I think he

stopped. He probably forgot to buy potato chips."

They crossed under the expressway and continued north, past furniture outlets, discount stores, and fried chicken shops. "We're really close," Joe said. He raised his head and looked along both sides of the road, then returned to the monitor. "Hey, we passed him! He's right here somewhere!"

Frank pulled onto the shoulder and stopped, then looked around. Across the road were a convenience store, a service station, and a garden supply shop. Nevins's car was not at any of them. He looked over his shoulder, at a seedy strip-shopping center. One movie theater, closed, a boarded-up supermarket, a rug and tile outlet—and a weathered sign that read Lots of Free Parking in the Rear.

"Joe," Frank said. "Go take a peek at the rear of that building. I'll stay with the van."

Moments later Joe hurried back, making an okay sign with his left hand. He put his head in the window and said, "He's there. And he's parked next to a door with a sign on it that says SysAlarmics."

"Get in, fast, and get down," Frank said. He had just caught sight of a car turning in at the shopping center. He couldn't be sure at that distance, but he had a strong impression that there were two or three people in the car. The guy at the wheel looked a lot like Hector from the HTH martial arts class.

The car disappeared behind the run-down building. "Surveillance time," Frank said after telling Joe what he had seen. From the locked cabinet in the back of the van, he took out a supersensitive parabolic microphone and a cassette recorder. Joe took the binoculars and a camera equipped with telephoto lens.

A clump of bushes at the back of the building offered a perfect hiding place. Frank hooked up the mike, put on earphones, and aimed the mike at an open window to the left of Nevins's car.

"Help it," a voice said.

Frank pressed the Record button.

"You'd better learn to help it," Nevins said coldly. "If anybody gets hurt on one of these jobs, the cops are going to work ten times harder to catch us. Now, let's go over our next objective. Vinnie?"

Frank's eyes widened. Vinnie was one of the robbers?

"Yeah, well," Vinnie said, "it's pretty much the same as usual. Tomorrow night we boost a car, and on Monday we wait until after ten-thirty to hit the bank. After we ditch the car, we come back here with the loot. Hey, Jack, when do we get our shares? My mom's birthday is coming up, and I want to get her a decent present."

"I told you," Nevins said. "Three jobs this week, and we're finished for good. We'll divide up the loot on Friday."

Joe suddenly grabbed Frank's arm and pointed toward the corner of the building. Another car had just come into view. It pulled up sharply, next to the office entrance, and Lisa Tang jumped out. Frank felt a jolt of disappointment. He had had a good feeling about the martial arts expert, and he was sorry to learn she was involved.

There was a bigger disappointment to come. The passenger in the car was Ricky. He rushed into the building. Over the headphones, Frank heard the office door open with a bang.

"What is this?" Nevins demanded.

In a voice shrill with fright, Ricky said, "I just saw Joe and Frank Hardy's van parked out by the road. They're onto us!"

Chapter

16

FRANK RIPPED OFF THE HEADPHONES and thrust
the cassette recorder into Joe's hands. "Take
the evidence and run for the van," he said.
"I'll try to slow them down."

It took Joe a split second to understand what
had happened. Then he jumped up and
sprinted across the parking area toward the
street. At that moment, the door to the building banged open. Hector, Lisa, and Vinnie
came running out.

"There he goes," Hector shouted. "Stop
him!"

Frank took a deep breath. This was not a
match, not a workshop. This was combat. He
set off at a run, on a course that intercepted

Hector's. Lisa's warning shout gave Hector just enough time to start to turn.

"Haii-ya!" Frank planted his left foot and launched a roundhouse foot-sword kick at Hector's neck. The blow caught him just under the ear and sent him staggering back into the wall.

Frank had no more time to waste on Hector. He spun around, just as Vinnie tried to dodge past him. Frank made a leap that put him between Vinnie and Joe's escape route, then waited in a semicrouch. Vinnie stopped, pulled a gravity knife from his pocket, and flicked it open. The summer sun sparkled on the edge of the blade.

"I don't want to cut you, Frank," Vinnie said, starting to circle to his right. "You saved my life the other day. I owe you one. But I got to get by you, whatever it takes."

"You're not getting by, Vinnie," Frank replied. "Give it up."

Most of Frank's attention was centered on Vinnie's knife. But he was also aware of Lisa, hovering in the background. Was she waiting for Vinnie to engage him, so that she could pursue Joe? Or did she intend to join Vinnie and gang up on him? And where was the rest of the gang—Jack Nevins, Ricky, and anyone else who might have been inside?

"Give it up, Vinnie," Frank repeated, circling to keep Vinnie between him and Lisa. "It's all over. Joe's already gotten away. He's on the cellular phone to the police right now. Don't make it any worse for yourself."

Vinnie's eyes flickered to Frank's right. Frank whirled around, just as Hector came charging at him, head down, fists windmilling. Frank hopped to one side, kicked him in the knee, and gave him a quick rabbit punch to the back of the neck. He went sprawling, right in the path of Vinnie's desperate attack. As Vinnie struggled to keep his balance, Frank brought the edge of his hand down on Vinnie's wrist. The knife went flying.

"No! Stop!" Lisa shouted.

Though tired and short of breath, Frank spun on one foot and crouched to face this latest and most dangerous attack, but Lisa wasn't talking to him. Jack Nevins was running for his car with a large suitcase in his left hand. Lisa took off after him.

A girl with dark hair burst through the doorway. Frank remembered seeing her in Lisa's martial arts class but didn't know her name. "He slugged Ricky and took the money," the girl shouted. "Look out, he's got a gun!"

Nevins slung the suitcase into the backseat of his sports car, then turned and pulled an automatic from his belt. "I'm leaving," he panted. "Don't try to stop me."

Lisa halted about six feet from him, knees bent. Her hands, held at arm's length, weaved a complicated pattern that Frank recognized from tai chi chuan. Was she really going to try to attack a man with a gun? That was suicide!

Vinnie's knife was on the pavement, just a couple of feet away. Frank made a lightning grab for it, held it by the point, and flung it in Nevins's direction. It spun end over end, catching the light. Nevins saw it coming out of the corner of his eye and flinched. As Frank had intended, the knife missed by a couple of feet, but that moment of inattention was enough. Lisa kicked the gun from Nevins's hand, then moved closer to deliver a devastating blow to his chest.

As Lisa whirled and stared at Frank with a level warrior's gaze, they heard the sound of sirens approaching from out on the road.

Lisa took a deep breath and straightened up. Then she pressed her palms together and bowed to Frank. He returned the salute as the first of the patrol cars came screaming around the corner of the parking lot.

"You mean, the whole scheme was put together by Jack Nevins?" Pat asked. It was the third time he had asked the question, and he still sounded as if he didn't believe the answer.

"That's right," Frank said. After he and Joe

had finished making their statements at police headquarters, they had joined Vanessa and Callie at Vanessa's house, then called Pat to come over.

Callie said, "I'm really happy you broke the case, guys. But the next time something like this comes along, you'd better not leave me out. Now explain it again—how did Nevins work it?"

"Lisa was the first person he recruited," Joe said. "He did it by promising to set her up with her own martial arts school. She saw a chance to fulfill her dream—and grabbed it."

"I guess I can understand that," Vanessa said slowly. "But how could she involve her students like that? When I think of little Ricky being part of a gang of armed criminals . . ."

Frank said, "According to Lisa, Ricky never took part in any of the holdups, except as a lookout. He wanted to—I guess waving a gun around would be like a super game of cops and robbers to him—but Lisa wouldn't let him."

"Then the actual bank robbers were Lisa and her three students?" Callie asked.

"That's right. Hector, Vinnie, and Melanie," Joe told her. "When Lisa found out that we were investigating the bank robberies, she was afraid that we had come to Hands to Help because we already suspected her. So she and her buddies decided to scare us off, or worse. It was Hector who hid in the supply room and tried to use my head for a baseball."

"He also tried to drop a cinder block through our windshield," Frank added.

"I suppose that cartoon was Ricky's work," Vanessa said. "I thought there was something childish about it at the time, but I didn't want to accuse anyone falsely."

"I don't know if we would have taken him seriously as a suspect anyway," Frank confessed. "I have to admit, I like him."

"Me, too," Joe said. "It's really a shame."

Pat cleared his throat. "After I got the word about all this," he said, "I spoke to someone I know at juvenile court. He couldn't promise anything, but he's going to keep a special eye on Ricky's case."

"I'm glad to hear that," Frank said. He was silent for a moment, then took up the tread of the story again. "When we weren't scared off, Lisa came up with the idea of framing us, by hiding some of the bank loot in our van, then phoning in an anonymous tip to the police. As far as she knew, it had worked. She was really shocked to see us show up this morning at the gang's headquarters."

Joe chuckled. "Not as shocked as she was when Nevins tried to bug out with most of the loot. I guess she never heard that saying about there being no honor among thieves."

Vanessa frowned. "One thing I don't understand," she said. "I thought all along that your chief suspect was Gil."

"He was," Joe replied. "And I'd still like to know why he went out of his way to pick on me."

"I think I can explain," Pat said. "Hands to Help means a lot to Gil, and so does his position as someone the younger kids look up to. He gets really angry when someone seems less than loyal to the program. And lately there's been more of that. People like Vinnie obviously don't feel the same kind of commitment Gil does. I don't know why he decided that you and Frank were to blame, but he did. So he tried to hit back. I was sorry I had to ask you two to leave the program, but it looked to me as if it was either you or Gil. And he really needs what we can give him."

"That makes sense," Frank said. "But you know, Pat, at that point we thought *you* were masterminding the bank holdups. We had already figured out that the robberies might be connected to Hands to Help. And then we saw you and Gil paying a visit to a gun dealer."

Pat stared. "You saw us?"

"We even got you on videotape," Joe said. "We couldn't think why you'd be there if you weren't involved in some kind of illegal activity. And just why *were* you there?"

"Gil heard a rumor about the guns and came to me with it," Pat replied. "I really saw red. So that very same day we went over and told the guy to get out of town. If he didn't, we were going to turn him in. I even said we had sworn statements from minors who had bought illegal weapons from him. I'm afraid that was stretching the truth a little bit, but he believed me. I don't think we'll be seeing him around here anymore."

"That guy was one tough customer," Joe said. "It must have taken a lot of guts to threaten him like that."

"Well, fortunately, both Gil and I have a lot of experience dealing with his type," Pat said.

Callie asked, "Pat, what's going to happen to your program now?"

He shook his head. "I wish I knew," he said. "We can survive without Jack Nevins's support. But can we survive once people learn how he corrupted the program and turned kids we were trying to help into gangsters? Who'll want to donate their money or volunteer their time to an organization that's under that kind of cloud?"

"Don't worry, Pat, *I'm* going to go right on working at HTH," Vanessa declared. She challenged Joe and Frank, "What about you guys?"

Frank shrugged. "I'm willing, if Pat needs me."

"Joe?" Vanessa asked.

"Well, I *was* thinking that it would be nice to take some time off and catch a few adventure flicks at the mall," Joe admitted.

Vanessa grabbed a cushion off the sofa and drew it at Joe.

With a grin, he quickly added, "But I guess I'll stick with Hands to Help. No matter how exciting a film is, how can it possibly match what we've been through the past few days?"

Frank and Joe's next case:

The New York State presidential primary is in full swing, and Nathan Webster, computer scientist turned independent candidate, is offering some exciting new ideas for the future. Frank and Joe are eager to hear his major campaign speech in Bayport. But Webster is also attracting a more sinister kind of attention ... a kind that could prove fatal! When a bomb disrupts Webster's Bayport appearance, the Hardys sign on as bodyguards—determined to ensure that the candidate can run for office without running into danger. But in protecting Webster, they too become targets of terror. And if Frank and Joe don't catch up with the stalker soon, they could all end up out of the race for good ... in *Campaign of Crime,* Case #103 in The Hardy Boys Casefiles™.

THE HARDY BOYS CASEFILES